Cavalry Recruit

**Center Point
Large Print**

**This Large Print Book carries the
Seal of Approval of N.A.V.H.**

Cavalry Recruit

WILL COOK

Macquarie
Regional Library

CENTER POINT PUBLISHING
THORNDIKE, MAINE

This Center Point Large Print edition
is published in the year 2006 by arrangement with
Golden West Literary Agency.

The text of this Large Print edition is unabridged. In other
aspects, this book may vary from the original edition. Printed in
Thailand. Set in 16-point Times New Roman type.

ISBN: 1-58547-868-7
ISBN 13: 978-1-58547-868-2

Library of Congress Cataloging-in-Publication Data

Cook, Will.
    Cavalry recruit / Will Cook.--Center Point large print ed.
      p. cm.
    ISBN 1-58547-868-7 (lib. bdg. : alk. paper)
    1. Large type books. I. Title.

  PS3553.O5547C35 2006
  813'.54--dc22

2006017092

Cavalry Recruit

1

Loch Angevine had never been able to decide which was worse—to be the oldest son or the youngest. The oldest was burdened with setting an example and the youngest was charged with following, and since he was not a leader, it was just as well that he was the youngest, although he was a poor follower.

Angus Angevine, the father, believed that characteristics were passed along in the family like a hunting case watch, and since his life had been bravely spent, he felt that courage, as well as the long, angular Angevine nose and the red hair, was as much a part of his youngest son as of the other three.

Perhaps it was the way of the Scots: they were people set in their ways, strong for the clan, and since Loch was the fourth son, he had been given a proud name. He somehow likened it to the launching of a ship whose course was predestined, yet he soon disappointed owner and builder by grounding himself on life's many shoals and forever dismasting himself by sailing recklessly in intemperate winds.

The first knowledge that he had that he was not up to the obligation of his name came when he was eleven and a horse stepped on his foot and he cried. His father was immeasurably shocked and showed it and thereafter watched him carefully, as though searching for some dread disease which might manifest itself at any moment.

7

Stuart, the oldest son, left home first and went to sea. He was followed by Robert, then Dundee, and after a few years they returned to the Ohio farm, strong in limb, steady and brave in the eye, and a pleasure to Angus Angevine.

Loch, at sixteen, was removed from school because it was time for him to go forth into the world and because he had had far too much schooling already. Because his brothers had gone to sea, Loch followed that example, took a train to New Bedford, and shipped out on a whaler. But the sea made Loch ill to the point where his usefulness was annulled and he was quickly put ashore in the pilot boat. The sea did not forge him. It melted him down, rendered him to his basic weaknesses, then disgorged him on the beach, less than when he began.

Returned home, Loch faced his father's gale-fury of disappointment and silently cursed the fate that had made him small in stature and courage. He was lectured by his father and brothers; they were unbelieving, shocked, stunned, and he listened, for he was a deaf man asked to hear music. He just did not understand what they wanted of him, what they prized so much.

Loch wanted to return to school where he could advance in mathematics and surveying and literature and history, for to him it seemed as though his mind were a crucible of unlimited capacity. And because there was nothing else to do with the boy, Angus Angevine agreed.

So while three brothers followed the winds of the sea, Loch posted fine marks at the academy, and these were viewed by his father as merely bookmarks in the pages of life, to be placed and forgotten.

In the year 1867, when Loch was twenty and still a slight man weighing no more than a hundred and forty-five pounds after a heavy meal, he finished his education. He was recognizably an Angevine, with the shock of red hair and the bony, prominent nose and the gray eyes, but he was an Angevine set apart.

He knew that he would never be a gentleman farmer like his father nor heroic sailing masters like his brothers. He had none of their desire to seek out foreign ports and faraway adventure and no desire to return periodically with their tales to spin.

Loch Angevine was a man who felt no calling at all, no desire to test himself, for he was neither satisfied with nor ashamed of what he was.

Yet his life couldn't be lived on his terms. On his twenty-first birthday, Loch Angevine was summoned to his father's study, given fifty dollars and a train ticket to Jefferson Barracks in Missouri, a reluctant blessing, and told to hie from the house and place himself in the care of the United States Army for four years.

"Begone from the glades and bookish ways," Angus Angevine told him. "Go into the army and take the measure of yourself, laddie. Search out yourself so that you'll become a man."

"What is it I search for?" Loch Angevine asked.

The older man waved his hand. "You will know it when you find it, and it will not be found in books. I came to this country with no money but with a will to make my place. This fine farm and all I have I owe to this country. You'll serve her now as your brothers serve her. Come back to me when you're your own man and my door will be open."

Loch Angevine understood the alternative. "What lies out there for me, father?"

"I know not. Go and find out and come back and tell me of it."

The sergeant's bull voice shook Loch Angevine free of his thoughts, and he rolled out of his bunk, tugged on his boots, and dashed out onto the parade ground with the rest of the company and fell in for inspection.

This was his third month at the barracks and his training was finished now. He was leaving and he wasn't sure whether he was excited about it or not. Standing in his place, an immovable man in a row of immovable men, Loch Angevine was not at all certain what he thought of the army. He remained rigid, eyes to the front while the sergeant and the lieutenant moved along, looking each man over carefully to pick up each flaw while the sergeant wrote it all down in the extra-duty book.

As they came into Loch's field of vision, he watched the sergeant, near fifty, with thirty years of army behind him and many battles done with; he was a hard man, often cruel, always just, and he had absolutely no compassion at all for anyone who did not shape up to his standard.

I must have that man for a friend, Angevine thought as the sergeant and the lieutenant stopped in front of him.

The lieutenant was young, no more than five years Angevine's senior, yet it was plain to the eye that the lieutenant had been forged in many fires. His face was blocky and stern, and his eyes were as impersonal as a pair of carbine barrels. A scar laced his left cheek and pulled the end of one eyebrow down, giving him a sardonic expression. Angevine thought that it would be nice to have a scar like that, and he wondered where the lieutenant had got it.

The lieutenant's critical eye went up and down; he would miss no flaw if any existed, and he found none. The sergeant stared, showing neither pleasure nor displeasure, yet Loch Angevine knew that a sloppy inspection would mean a dressing down for the sergeant in the lieutenant's office, and the sergeant would come out with thunder on his face and they'd feel the wrath all that day.

But the inspection went well; out of the entire company, only five men drew extra punishment and that would take the form of guard duty because the company was marching that day, leaving Jefferson for New Mexico and Arizona Territory.

The company was ready to dismiss. The sergeant and the lieutenant faced each other properly and the lieutenant said, "I want to see Palmer, Nordeen,

Wilkes, and Angevine in my office in five minutes, sergeant."

There was an exchange of precise salutes and then the lieutenant strode off, very erect, as though the bones of his spine had been fused. His heels chopped the dust and then the sergeant repeated the lieutenant's order; they always did that, as though the troops were deaf. But it was a form and it was always followed exactly.

They were dismissed and the four men ordered to report looked at each other and wondered what hidden sin had been turned up to light; a private was not summoned for anything less than a serious matter.

In the headquarters orderly room they sat rigidly on the hard chairs and tried not to notice the captains and majors and other officers who flitted about on their very important business. Loch Angevine observed them carefully without drawing attention to that fact. He had noticed that when two privates walked from one point to another, they talked and laughed and you could just look at them and tell that they weren't going anywhere in particular, and if they were, they weren't going to do anything important when they got there.

But an officer, even a second lieutenant, seemed always bound toward some exciting destiny, driven by some fervent purpose, and stamped by some knowing, unseen hand for future greatness. Not tomorrow perhaps, but someday. They all seemed aware of this and carried themselves especially carefully as though their responsibility were fragile and had to be preserved for that one moment when their name would be a rallying cry, when they would leap forward and lead and fall, but forever be remembered because they had led and fallen.

Loch Angevine watched all the officers carefully, for he felt that there, above all, he would find the answers he hungered for.

"Angevine," the orderly said brusquely and he was on his feet, moving through the doorway into the cave of his leader, Lieutenant Bascomb, into the throne room where his leader sat and contemplated the crushing weight of command.

"Close the door and sit down," Bascomb said and motioned Angevine to a chair.

The office was a disappointment, just a small room with a pine desk, one table, a map on the wall, and three chairs. No displayed weapons wrested from the fallen. No bleached bones of the conquered.

Angevine sat down and looked at the lieutenant, who said, "I had your record from the recruiting office brought here, Angevine. You're an educated man."

He said it as though it were an amazing thing and he could hardly get over it, and to cover his concern he thumbed through several sheets of paper. "You have a college education, Angevine. Why didn't you apply for a commission?"

"I don't think I could lead men, sir."

The lieutenant frowned and the scar puckered; this was not the answer he expected, or wanted. "Angevine, did you leave any felonies behind you?"

"No, sir."

"A woman then?"

"No, sir."

The lieutenant, a man with limited patience, slapped the desk heartily. "Damn it, you just can't have a college education in the ranks! It's not good. Not good at all."

Angevine had disturbed the lieutenant, the man who, above all, he did not want to disturb. The officer stared at him, then said, "You've been a good recruit, Angevine. Good attention to duty. I hope you won't disappoint me, Angevine."

"In what way, sir?"

"A man doesn't have to be smart to follow orders, Angevine, and it's been my experience that an intelligent, educated man tends to ask 'why' too often to make a good soldier. I'll be keeping my eye on you, that's all. Dismissed."

There was an exchange of salutes, an about-face, and Angevine walked out, baffled and a bit hurt, for he felt that he was being preblamed for mistakes he hadn't yet made. Yet it was a challenge, what he had joined for, to serve, to be brave and honorable, and to discover for himself what was obviously so precious to other men.

The lieutenant did not trust him. Therefore Loch Angevine must, by his devotion to duty, his attention and flawless performance, show the lieutenant that he could be trusted. There was the challenge, to make this man understand that he was capable of doing more than was required of him.

Sergeant Gore was waiting for him at the barracks.

"What the hell have you been up to?" Gore wanted to know, showing Angevine his native suspicions of all private soldiers. He put out his hand and pushed against Angevine's chest, and when he was backed against the wall, Gore held him there. "I've been watchin' you, mister. How come you ain't got drunk at the sutler's?"

When Loch Angevine dredged his mind for a reason and opened his mouth to give it, Gore said, "Never mind. What did the lieutenant want to see you about?"

"We talked about my education, sergeant."

There was no mercy in Gore at any time and even less when he looked intently into Angevine's eyes. "Oh, that. You ain't in trouble, are you? I don't want a man who's in trouble. There'll be plenty of it where we're goin' and I need none in my company. You do your work, see. You do it right because I'll be keepin' an eye on you." He took his hand off Angevine's chest and stopped pressing him against the wall. "You understand me?"

"Yes, sergeant."

Gore nodded once, his expression not changing. "I'm goin' to make a soldier out of you. Understand?"

"Yes, sergeant. I want to be a good soldier."

"Ah, do you now?"

"Yes. I want to be like you, sergeant."

The suspicion again; it came back in a rush, strong in his eyes, and his manner turned threatening.

15

"Makin' fun of me, are you? I can teach you not to ever do that."

"But I wasn't," Angevine protested. "I want to be like you, sergeant. I want to be brave, sergeant."

"You'll soon have your chance once we hit the Apache country," Gore said. "If you're lucky, you'll live, and if you're alive when our work is done, you'll be brave. The ones that ain't are soon dead." He tapped Angevine on the chest with his finger, and it felt like the blunt end of a stick and hurt him a little, but he let none of this show on his face. "Every man in my company is a hero, Angevine. If he ain't, I get rid of him. Understand?"

"Yes, I do, sergeant. I want to stay in your company."

"Ah, you won't find it easy. All this drillin' and such is play compared to what it'll be."

"That's all right."

Gore nodded. "Take care then 'cause I'll be watchin'." He turned and left and Angevine watched him leave and then he let out a long sighing breath and rubbed the spot on his chest where Gore had jabbed him with his finger.

That night they got everything ready, horses, mules, wagons, arms and ammunition and surveying equipment, and there were endless inspections by officers who seemed eternally dissatisfied with progress or the way this was done or that was packed. Nothing must be forgotten or broken or lost; they would be nine hundred miles from the nearest base of supply and

16

deep into hostile Indian country and nothing must be left to chance.

Angevine's duty would be to survey land and he was in charge of two pack mules and the equipment they carried, as well as his personal gear, arms, and supplies. He supposed that this was not as demanding a duty as the cavalry who went along for protection, but he believed that it was as important. The cavalrymen were a clannish, snobbish lot and looked down on any soldier from another branch, and Angevine supposed this was the way all mounted men felt, surveying everything around them from the advantageous height of the saddle.

This superiority, he had noticed, trudged up through the ranks to the sergeants and to the officers; the cavalry lieutenants were a gay, dashing lot and rather sneered at the others, even Lieutenant Bascomb, who resented it no end and was determined to conduct his company so well that he would never have to ask the cavalry for any assistance whatsoever. The cavalrymen were inclined to take liberties with their uniform, and the more bizarre they became, the more proper did Bascomb's troops appear. It was a contest of extremes.

Thus Loch Angevine had learned that perfection was the only ultimate weapon against the opinion of others and was the great oil in calming the disturbed seas of life. The army did not make mistakes, and because Angevine was now a functioning part of the army, he would by the same token be making no mistakes, and this pleased him, to be above criticism.

Their departure early the next morning was a spectacle. The general was there with his magnificent white horse and a blue blanket cut to fit over the saddle; it had yellow piping around it and two stars sewn onto it so that the general could be identified from afar. He was a short man with a goatee and a dense mustache, and he took great liberty with his uniform, for his shirt was a red and white candy stripe and he wore a flowery tie. The general rode his white horse around and made comments here and there to the officers; he appeared not to notice the enlisted men at all, except for a few sergeants he had served with and with these men he exchanged neutral pleasantries while they stood at stiff attention.

The newspapers and magazines had sent reporters and photographers by the dozens, and the photographers set up their equipment and wagons along the line of march and made ready to record on ground glass the immortal image of this great adventure.

Civilians drove for days, covering many miles, just to see this mass of troops on the march, and many of the soldiers had wives who tearfully said goodbye.

Children and dogs ran about unchecked, constantly in the way and underfoot. They made the horses and mules restless and finally several of the cavalry troops rounded them up and shooed them elsewhere to play.

Amid all this there was a rising, dense pall of dust and the heat was strong and there was a good deal of noise. But it was not confusion, Loch Angevine assured himself; the army would not permit it.

A cavalry trumpeter blew the command and the foot soldiers, resentful of this mounted superiority, had the same call repeated in the infantry key of G; it was a minor aggravation, expressed in a minor way, yet it seemed to be a harbinger of the basic discontent and rivalry and petty jealousy that is fermented by the promotional list and rival services.

The cavalry was the first in motion, the point riders parading from the post with carbine butts planted on their thighs, angled just so, hats boxed low over their eyebrows; they looked as though they were going to do battle any moment and were not at all afraid. Flankers went out as soon as they cleared the post, and the foot soldiers, the infantry companies, the engineers, and artillery marched and lumbered along in the cavalry dust.

It took forty minutes to clear the post, to clear the waving of handkerchiefs and the children and dogs running after them, but they did draw clear and set a course to the southwest, facing now a seemingly limitless rolling prairie with buffalo grass stirring in the breeze.

Then it was thirty miles a day, with housekeeping and rest stops at the proper intervals, and each night a camp, properly set up, with company streets and command posts. While the foot soldiers rested, the cavalry stood guard in shifts, taking in the whole perimeter of the camp while each company posted their security walks, sixty paces one way and sixty back with a 'who goes there' for anyone caught strolling about.

There were streams to ford and rivers to cross, and in ten days they were deep into the vastness of the Indian country, and each day the cavalry scouts reported seeing Indians far out there on their ponies, surely thinking that here were more white men than they ever knew existed.

They were in buffalo land and all one day and one night they were forced to halt while a massive herd passed in front of them, making the very ground tremble and the sky dark with the raised dust. For several days everyone talked about it and wondered if they dared tell anyone back home about it for fear that they would be put down as monumental liars.

Anyone in his right mind would know that there were just not that many buffalo.

A large party of Indians approached the marching columns and indicated that they wanted to parley. Angevine was glad to get the rest, yet he would liked to have had a closer look at the conference being held on the prairie.

The cavalry major had a tent pitched and flags and guidons planted and a table and chairs set up, and a to-do was made of the whole thing. The band played several selections and the artillery officer fired his piece three times, which frightened the Indians a little, but pleased them.

There was some discussion between the cavalry major and the infantry major as to who would preside over the meeting. They settled it, as all official disputes are settled, on the seniority basis, the infantry major being the longest in grade.

This was a bit unfortunate because he had some peculiar ideas about Indians, notions based on no direct knowledge, and he was too proud a man to accept advice. Of course the Indians wanted rifles to hunt buffalo with, but the major—his name was Halstead—knew that the Indians really wanted the weapons so they could massacre white settlers, and he refused to give them any. He also refused to give them powder and shot or anything to eat or to drink, and then he seemed offended when the Indians expressed a disenchantment with him.

The parley ended, with the major's suspicions of Indians renewed and the Indians' suspicions of the white man renewed, and the Indians rode away and the column marched on.

But that night word traveled down from Halstead that the foot guard would be doubled and every man would be alert to imminent attack.

Loch Angevine drew guard duty from two to four in the morning and he didn't grumble about it. As a matter of fact, he had not complained about anything at all—not about the dust or the poor food or the rate of march—and the corporal had noticed this and told Sergeant Gore, who told Lieutenant Bascomb, and they talked it over and just knew that he was up to something.

Angevine's duty tour was the customary sixty paces

and at each end he met, before turning about, the guard on the other tour. And this was the way it went, up and down between the tents, correct cadence, rifle on the shoulder, a position of arms-carrying that was disgusting to a cavalryman.

While he was halfway down his tour, there was a sudden whoop, a warbling flapping of the hand over the mouth, followed by the boom of a .68 caliber rifle and a man's choked cry. The guards on either side of Angevine bolted their position and ran toward the sound of the shot, and he even started to do that, but he remembered, ported his weapon, and bellowed for the corporal of the guard, who was already dashing that way.

He did not leave his post until properly relieved, then went toward the crowd that had gathered around to see what had happened. Pushing his way through, he saw that it was no Indian at all but a cavalryman who had been set on putting a scare into those 'plow pushers.'

That one war whoop had cost him his lower jaw because the frightened guard had fired without really looking, and the bullet had torn away half the man's face.

The contract surgeon was there and three men held the screaming cavalryman to the ground while the surgeon tried to staunch the bleeding and get him onto a litter and over to the wagons. Loch Angevine, now that he had seen, wished that he hadn't and felt quite sick to his stomach. He walked back to his tent and turned into his blankets and tried to sleep, but it was useless. Even though the surgeon's wagons were far back, the man's cries could be heard throughout the night.

Just before dawn they stopped.

2

A burial detail was organized, a grave dug, a squad assembled, and the cavalryman was buried on the prairie. A marker was placed over his grave and one of the officers read a short service. Afterward the cavalry major did a lot of shouting and proclaimed his desire to 'get to the bottom of this sorry mess' and the whole march was delayed a day while the major looked into it.

The infantry laughed and agreed that they'd get a lot of rest if they shot one of the cavalry bastards every other night. The joke went around the camp, as jokes do, and Loch Angevine heard it and didn't think it was funny, but he repeated it because it was the thing to do.

The cavalry major was holding forth in his tent and he took the officers to task first; one could hear him venting his temper, now and then cursing. All the officers, when they left his tent, jerked their kepis down hard over their heads and dug their heels in when they walked. Their faces were stone and everyone knew that no good would come of this.

The soldier who had fired the fateful shot was under close guard and he worried a lot because it looked as though he'd be hung for this; the cavalry major acted as though a personal attack had been made on his honor and he wanted everyone to understand that his men could not be shot that way and nothing be done about it.

Loch Angevine was summoned at last because he was a witness to the whole thing. As he approached the tent, he felt himself tremble slightly; it was like approaching his father's study for one of life's miserable lessons, an inquiry into the why and wherefore of his tardy manhood.

Lieutenant Bascomb was there, outside. He said, "Tell the truth, Angevine. You have nothing to fear."

Angevine gave him a fleeting smile, then wondered if that instant of familiarity would be remembered and held against him. An orderly parted the tent flap, and he stepped inside and faced a table with a grim row of officers behind it.

He gave them his smartest salute and had it returned. He was not invited to sit.

The cavalry major mopped his sweating brow because the tent was hot and the flies buzzed around and he was continually swatting at them. One landed on Angevine's face and dug in for a meal. As he raised his hand, the major barked: "You're at attention, soldier!"

He stared at Angevine as though warning him never to do that again.

24

And Angevine held his cheek rigid as the fly dined.

"You were walking a guard tour when the incident took place," the major said. "Relate what happened. Be brief."

"The cavalry soldier whooped like an Indian and the guard fired, sir."

The major stared and the other officers stared and then the major said, "Well?"

"I was brief, sir."

A captain chuckled and drew a glare from the major that would have cost him three places on the promotion list had he been cavalry. The infantry major, who was inclined to overweight and irritability, said, "Hoskins, it's hot as hell and we've been at this three hours now. I know you lost a man, but he did a damned foolish thing and he paid dearly. It's unreasonable for a guard to ask a man's rank and serial number before shooting. So I suggest, with all due respect, sir, that in the future you curb the exuberance of your troopers while the guards walk the inner perimeter. This *is* hostile country." He gathered up his cigar case and kepi and gloves, and three other officers rose with him. The cavalry major scowled but knew that it was over and it had come to nothing.

"You're dismissed, soldier," he said. "This damned hearing is dismissed."

The infantry major looked at him, nodded, and went out with his retinue. Loch Angevine managed a salute and an about-face and got out of the tent. He was walking away when Sergeant Gore came up from the rear and took his arm.

"Let's have a little talk, laddie." He steered him aside and then stopped, still holding his arm. "I want to tell you that you did well last night, stayin' to your post the way you did. It's damned sure saved you some extra duty." He grinned. "I like a man who can think on his feet."

"Thank you, sergeant."

"I said I'd be keepin' me eye on you, didn't I? And I will, laddie." He released Angevine's arm. "It's not often I find a recruit with his wits about him, and when I do, he'll bear watchin'."

"Sergeant, what do I do wrong?"

"Not a thing, laddie, and I'll tell you that in my thirty some years as a soldier I've yet to see that kind of a private. It makes you a bit hard to understand, laddie."

"I don't want to disappoint you, sergeant. That's the last thing I want to do." He reached out impulsively and touched Gore, and the sergeant opened his eyes a little wider and looked at the hand until it was removed. "I only have four years on my enlistment and I want to learn, sergeant. No matter what you want done, I'll volunteer. You don't even have to ask me; I'll be ready when you say."

Gore stepped back as though he had just discovered that Angevine was the carrier of a communicable disease. "Volunteer? Shirkin' duty I can understand, but volunteerin'?" He shook his head and backed up a

26

step. "Aw, I'll be keepin' a close eye on you, laddie. You're a strange one."

The army moved on in its regulated, precise manner, across the plains of gamma grass and across endless small creeks and rivers, marking its passage by twice accidentally setting the prairie afire and twice furiously fighting to bring it under control.

And the Indians kept close watch over the marching men, but there was no attack because the artillery captain conducted his practice firing on those days when the Indians appeared in the distance and thereby impressed them with the white man's superiority, at least when it came to killing in large numbers.

And the Indians massed as many as they could until at times there were a thousand mounted warriors, for they were human too and took pride in man's greatest accomplishment, his capacity to make war.

Of course the artillery officer felt that the presence of his muzzle loaders held the enemy at bay, and the cavalry, inclined by nature to be proud and arrogant, swore that their mounted flankers deterred the savages, while the infantry major brushed this all aside and declared that only fools would ignore the might of his dismounted men delivering enfilade fire.

By the time the troops reached the Canadian River as it moved into the mountains of New Mexico, the officers were eating at their separate messes and talking to each other only when duty demanded it.

Fort Union was a pleasant surprise, for instead of

being a crude, primitive post it was orderly and comfortable. Laid in a valley and buttressed by mountains, the officers' row was an avenue of twelve identical buildings, adobe built, with hipped roofs and a wide, sheltered porch facing a windbreak of good trees. The buildings were separated by fifteen feet of clear space, yet a boardwalk connected each. At the far end, the commander's quarters rose elegantly to two stories.

Behind the officers' row, set at an angle were other buildings of adobe, with tiled roofs. The married enlisted men were to occupy these. The parade ground, a huge stretch of real estate, separated the quarters from headquarters, supply, stable, farrier yard, and other storage buildings.

There was no palisade nor was there a need for one. Any attack would have to originate in the high, rough, weathered rocks that made up the face of the mountains and would also have to cross much open ground before reaching the post buildings.

Loch Angevine, billeted with the platoon of engineers, did not think anything at all about the post. He did not consider it a poor place because he had never been to such a place before and had nothing to compare it with. At the same time he did not think of it as being grand because this was his first real station and the location was more important to him than the comforts.

The cavalry, officers and enlisted men, soon occupied the best quarters and barracks on the post, and the artillery detachment, being a cut above the infantry, took second best.

There was no third best and the infantry camped in tents just south of the stable area. It was a sad choice for the prevailing winds carried to them a near constant aroma of manure and ammonia.

Angevine's first concern was what the soldiers called 'settling in,' getting to know the post, weathering out a payday and getting drunk at the sutlers' store. Only after this period were they really prepared for duty and the officers knew it.

The paymaster was eight days overdue and the officers began to worry about it. Finally the cavalry major sent his best captain and a half company out to see what the devil was holding the man up.

This detail left, was out three and a half days, and then came back with the paymaster's wagon, loaded with what the Apaches had left, and presented the burying detail with a nasty job of sorting it all out and getting them underground. Heat, time, carrion, and the natural decaying process left only unpleasantness, and the bodies were taken out of the wagon with scoop-shovels and put directly into the pine caskets.

The cavalry major was in a fury over this tragedy and wanted to organize a large force to run down the Indians and punish them, but the officers who had been on station at the post persuaded him finally that the guilty Indians were long gone and no trace would ever be found of them.

Besides, their civilian guide, Holly, was in Taos

indulging himself in the fandango houses, for he had three months' pay in his pocket, ten days' leave, and a great yearning for women and whisky.

So the paymaster and his detail were buried and the cavalry major turned his attention to the job at hand, the establishment of a military telegraph line between Fort Union and the boom-bustling town of Silver City, a mighty far piece to the southwest.

In truth, Lieutenant Bascomb and his men were going to build the telegraph, which was to say that they would survey the route, design the relay stations, and the cavalry and infantry would go along and guard the workers and camps.

The cavalry major never liked to think of it in this light; he had his own perspective on just about everything. But, whatever he thought of it, the job had to be done and the summer was in full heat and the general expected the line to carry messages in the late fall.

If it did not, the cavalry major might just as well look for a comfortable front porch somewhere because he would soon be retiring.

Because he was a surveyor, Loch Angevine was under Sergeant Gore's direct command, which suited him just fine. The survey detail consisted of twenty-six men, sixteen pack mules, twelve horses, and a squad of cavalry for an escort. They left the post on Wednesday, June 3, 1868. The mission and growing town of Santa Fe was their destination and the cavalry major felt that they could survey this piece and set poles and string line without the services of the civilian scout.

Telephone poles by the hundred, which had been freighted in from a saw camp near Pueblo, Colorado, were loaded onto wagons, and the work began. Two and a half miles a day; they were out of sight of the post by the first nightfall, leaving behind a line of gaunt poles with two glass insulators on them and wire running back, shining copper in the last of the sunlight.

Sergeant Gore and his detail of twelve men were six miles beyond and camped in a desolate nest of rocks with a spring nearby. A five-man cavalry detail had their cook-fire a short distance away, and Loch Angevine could hear them talking in low, amused tones.

He filled his mess tin and went off by himself to eat, content to be alone and pleased that he was left alone. He did not really know any of the men in the detail—he knew their names but he did not know them. He supposed that he might never know them because a man should know himself first before he put his attention on other men.

The vastness of the country left him with an uneasy feeling, yet he didn't believe that he was particularly afraid. Through his survey instrument the distance was brought close to him. After the work of the day was done, he took the telescope and put it in the case and then in his pocket; and before it got fully dark, he climbed to a large rock and, until the light was gone, studied the broken sweep of the land.

He wondered why anyone would want to come to this land; there didn't seem to be anything out there but mountains and desert. Yet he had come to it, for reasons of his own, so he questioned it no further.

They reached Sante Fe with their poles and wire and there was a lot of excitement over this. People in the town celebrated with a large feast and dancing, and Loch Angevine wondered why they carried on like that because they hadn't done so much. The town was much larger than he expected, but it was on the main trail for travelers to California and there were many wagons there and many people with their families and all they possessed. As he walked around he could hear the talk, the nasal twang of New England and the soft slur of Georgia and the brittle hardness of Iowa and Illinois.

But he had no interest in the town or the people and he wanted only to get on with his work.

Sergeant Gore, who was in charge, seemed in no hurry, and they remained in Sante Fe for two days and three nights, which was enough time for the cavalry detail to get drunk and into trouble with the local citizens. By the time Gore gathered his party, loaded the pack mules, and got ready to leave, the citizens and merchants stood sullenly by and watched, glad to see them going, for the soldiers had had their way with the women and bullied a few men and broken some windows and generally worn out their welcome.

They moved south-southwest with transom and

stick, days on end of mountains and valleys and summer heat and insects which brought the bad temper in men close to the surface, like blood, ready to flow at the slightest scratch.

For days they followed the Rio Grande valley, driving their stakes. Now and then they shot game for the evening meal as their diet was monotonous, something they could continually complain about.

Loch Angevine could not fail to notice that the soldiers found little to their liking. The weather was too hot and the insects were bad and the dust was intolerable and the terrain was either too flat or too hilly or too brushy or too rocky and they wanted a bath, yet they complained when there was a creek to cross. The coffee was either too strong or too weak, the beans done too well or not done enough.

Angevine could find no single person who thought that anything was all right, and it made him wonder about himself, for he could not find anything particularly bad. The weather *was* hot and the insects *were* bothersome and all this walking and climbing was difficult until a man toughened up to it. The food was poor, but they had to carry everything and could not expect biscuits and pan gravy.

As they moved southward into the parched, desert reaches, the talk turned to Indians; they discussed the possibility of attack constantly, and there was not an Indian depredation, fact or fancied, that wasn't recounted in endless detail. Angevine, having no experience at all with Indians, kept out of the conversations and merely sat there and listened, trying to separate truth from lies.

He did not feel uneasy because he was in Indian country nor alarmed at the prospect of trouble, and he supposed that this was because he could not really comprehend the horror of Indian torture or the lingering agony of Indian captivity. His lack of knowledge shielded him and he wondered if he should be grateful or not.

As he listened to the talk, he became aware that every man in the survey party, save himself, had had experience with the Indians. Every man, by his own admission, was a hero, and some had been heroes several times over. He alone had not tasted blood or met the enemy face to face and this made him feel very inadequate. Several of the cavalry troopers admitted that they had, during prior service with the Republic of Texas, engaged in hand to hand combat to the death with the infamous Comanches.

Yet it was a comfort to Loch Angevine to be in the company of these men, and he counted himself lucky to have joined a survey party where every man was a bona fide hero. Surely, when trouble came to them, he would have examples of how to conduct himself and his only hope was that he would not bring disgrace to himself.

They were soon surveying in the deep desert, miles of eye-aching brightness under a vertical sun, broken only by stunted brush and windblown hollows and bare rocks thrust up like cathedrals here and there.

Strange hot winds blew and the nights turned cold. There was no shelter save their small tents, and Sergeant Gore rationed the drinking water, with only a little to spare for cooking and none at all for washing.

For the last two days, Angevine had peered through his telescope to the furthermost chimney rocks and had seen smoke. When he told Gore of this, the sergeant brushed it aside, saying it was wind devils lifting dust, and because Gore said that, Angevine was not disturbed, for he had been in this country long enough now to know that the wind and the sun played strange tricks.

The Apaches struck their camp just before dawn, when the bowl of the sky was gray and only a rosy flush pushed it back to the east. They came with no warning at all, and the cavalry soldier on duty at the picket line fell with a bullet through his breastbone. The camp was in an instant uproar, for the Apaches had come in on their bellies, completely silent, and they were in the camp, shooting, knifing.

Loch Angevine came out of his tent, a cap-and-ball Remington in hand, but before he could cock and fire, an Apache knife plunged into his back and he fell, still conscious, but unable to move.

He lay sideways on the ground, a witness to it all and bitterly aware that any movement meant death. Sergeant Gore and the others tried to make a fight of it, but Angevine judged that no more than five shots were gotten off at the Apaches and he couldn't see that they'd been hurt at all.

In less than a minute the survey party was done in and the cavalry detail killed trying to protect the horses. Angevine lay like a dead man, too filled with pain to move, and too frightened to try.

The Apaches, numbering no more than ten, ran about, looting the camp of arms and ammunition and taking the greatest prize of all, the horses and mules. They went from body to body and stripped off what clothing they wanted, taking canteens, ammunition, watches, brass buttons, and insignia.

One approached Angevine, bent so close that Angevine could smell his stink while Angevine, eyes wide open, looked steadily across the patch of carnage his vision included. Fortunately, he too passed for dead.

The Apache was not large, but he was superbly muscled and was completely naked except for a loin leather and wrap-around leggings. His face was broad, with thick lips and a flat, bony nose. The eyes were like chocolate drops, and as expressionless.

The Remington, still gripped in Angevine's hand, was torn free, and all the time Angevine kept his eyes fixed straight ahead, determined not to cry out in pain if he were moved. Roughly the Apache stripped Angevine of powder flask and shot pouch. He also took the buttons off his uniform and his kepi, then walked away to join the others who were looting the camp.

Angevine expected them to leave then, but they did

not. Instead they killed one of the mules, built a fire, and spent half the day eating and jabbering in their guttural talk.

The dead drew the flies and the sun beat down on him, making his head swim and finally he fainted away and when he woke it was night and the fire was dead and the Apaches were gone.

The desert lost the heat of the day quickly and a chill wind husked down, blowing sand and dirt, and now Angevine tried to move, dragging himself painfully about, a flame roaring in his flesh where the Apache knife had torn him.

He reached one man and found him stiff, then crawled to another, and another; they were all dead, all these heroes dead and it didn't seem right that he should still be alive.

The Apaches had taken everything—blankets, rope, food, guns, knives, horses, and what was not taken had been smashed. The surveying equipment was a shambles, except for the telescope which was still in the case in Angevine's pocket. They had missed it, he supposed, because he had been lying on it when the Apache had stripped him of ammunition.

He could not remain: this he knew, because the vultures would arrive with the sun. And it was an uninhabitable spot—no water, no shelter. It was suitable only for dying, and Loch Angevine was not dead yet. However, it came to him that he soon would be if he did not find water and shelter.

He was not sure that he could walk but he was deter-

37

mined to try, and with much pain and effort he managed to get to his feet and by some miracle he did not immediately fall. One arm, his right, was not much use to him because the Apache knife had cut enough muscle to cause him great pain in that arm.

A few steps assured him that he could move about, and he sat down and tried to think things out. To stagger off into the desert with no cover for his head, no water to drink, no weapon to defend himself with would be the same as dying here.

He considered his problem, the gravity of the situation, and then made his decision. He was too weak to move much and he had to rest often, but he did not give in to the pain or his weakness and each effort seemed to make him stronger.

He gathered the damaged pots and pans and all the mess trays and laid them on the ground to collect the dew. And he found a broken knife, the tip gone, but four inches of sharp blade remaining. This he stuck in his belt. He had his telescope and compass and he found some matches the Apaches had missed and put all these things in his pocket.

Then he rested, dozing, dreaming horribly, waking with a start, and fear a tearing sensation in his chest. Finally dawn came and he stirred himself and gathered up his tins and carefully poured the condensed dew into a gallon pot. It added up to quite a bit and he drank some of it and felt better.

Then he gathered the trays and pans and made a bundle of them. Carrying his pot of water he struck a direction by compass and staggered away from this place where the dead lay waiting for the buzzards and the coyotes to dine.

When the sun became hot and nearly unbearable, he stopped and filled one large pot with sacaton grass and clapped it on his head like some ancient helmet. This insulated him from the brain-boiling heat.

His concern was with direction, going back along the survey line, and he was determined not to fall and spill his water, which he carried carefully, both hands gripping the bale. The pain was with him still, but he knew he could stand that.

Behind him, some miles now because he moved with relentless determination, buzzards swooped down. He looked once, then moved on and never looked back again.

3

Eight miles was the distance he traveled that first day and each step he paid for in pain, but he did not fall and did not spill his water. When the sun went down, he still lived which was a miracle of determination.

Angevine could not say how badly he had been hurt but he was positive that no vital organs had been reached by the knife. Perhaps some bone had deflected the blow; he didn't know and it really didn't matter to him.

He was alive and the others were dead, all those

heroes gone in one fell swoop, and he had to stay alive, to get back and report the exact details of it to Lieutenant Bascomb who would be hard put to understand how it happened.

It would be difficult to explain, Angevine knew, how all these men could die and not one Apache fall. Somehow it seemed shameful to say a thing like that, as though they had all been fools and had been taken in completely.

With his telescope, Angevine bellied down and studied the land carefully. He was on high ground, with a good view of a valley and he carefully looked it over. There seemed to be a game trail farther down and he observed several deer moving along it as though going to some hidden destination. He watched while the light began to fade, then decided that the deer were going to some water hole. He had heard somewhere that animals did that, and when he thought about it, he realized that the Apaches had to have water too, so he put away the telescope, gathered his pans, fought his way to his feet and went to investigate.

His intentions were not so easily executed, for the light was failing and he had to move slowly because of the pain and because he dared not spill what water he had left, and the trail was some distance, farther than he had thought. Angevine worked his way down the rocky flank, reached the trail, and followed it for what seemed like three-quarters of a mile until it ended in a small seep, a basin in the rocks not three

40

feet in diameter but filled with water that dripped from some crevices in the rock wall.

The animals that had been drinking scattered long before he got there and he could see by the dampness that the animals had lowered the water level. Probably they drank it dry each evening and then it filled up again, drop by drop.

He took the two largest kettles—one he had been wearing for a hat—and he filled them and set them aside. Then he bathed his face and head in the water and considered sitting in it to soak, but he decided that might start the bleeding again and settled for just washing his face.

After drinking all he wanted, Loch Angevine thought that this would be a good place to hole up and get some of his strength back. He was hungry beyond belief, but he knew he could live awhile without food. He needed the water.

Still, if he remained at the seep, the animals would be frightened away and they'd die and the thought bothered him, that he could be responsible for their deaths. Had he not seen them along the trail, he would not have found this water. He owed his life to them, so he climbed a good distance away and found a pocket in the rocks and settled there to endure the cold night. His pain was constant and kept him awake for long stretches of time, but then weariness dulled it and he would drift off and dream horrible dreams and wake with a start, not sure whether his delirium was real or not.

The dawn sun arrived, although he had thought for a time that it never would. Somehow he felt better and the gnawing in his stomach was now only an ache and he could ignore that. Returning to the water hole, he found it nearly dry and there were tracks all around where animals, driven by thirst, had overcome their fear of the man scent he had left about. Angevine still had his two kettles of water and he started out again, down the trail marked by survey stakes, but he kept to the high ground where the rocks hid him much of the time. He felt it too dangerous to travel on the open ground.

Without the kettle to put on his head, the climbing sun began to bother him, so he took off his shirt and made an Arab burnoose of it and he immediately felt better.

The urge to stop, to rest, to sit was always strong in him, and at times it almost overpowered him, so he devised a game to keep himself going. He took the march ten steps at a time, telling himself that he would take ten steps and then sit down, and on the tenth step he'd tell himself that he had to take ten more. He offered himself various prizes for doing this. Take ten more and he won a free gold mine, another ten, the hand of a French can-can dancer who was really a duchess incognito; his near-delirium carried him far that day, drove him a distance of eighteen miles.

He knew this distance was accurate because he was a surveyor, a man accomplished in mathematics, and he knew the distance between the survey markers and how many he had passed. By his estimation, the line crew and pole setters ought to be another day and a half away, if he could continue this pace, and he believed he could.

During the day he had consumed one pot of the water; he had one remaining, a little more than a gallon, and he figured that he could conserve it enough to take him through.

His feet were giving out, for the sand had eaten through the thread that stitched his shoes together; they were coming apart and he wondered whether or not he should take them off and go it barefoot. Then through a gap between sole and upper he saw that his socks were bloody and he knew that his feet were in bad shape and better off with some kind of covering.

So he took off his pants and with the knife, cut them in long strips and bound his feet tightly. This felt good, refreshing, and he laughed softly because he had found a chip of pleasantness floating in a sea of misery.

That night he slept reasonably well and was up and moving again at the first flush of dawn, still carrying carefully his last pot of water.

The sun was not as bright as it had been. He saw that a layer of high scud clouds filtered the scalding rays and he thought that maybe there was some bad weather in the making. It might even rain because he had heard some of the soldiers say that it was not impossible at this time of the year to get a flash flood.

Rain, he thought, might be a relief.

But it never came.

In the late afternoon all the clouds were gone and the sun died in a wild burst of color. After it had disappeared beyond the horizon, the grayness of twilight seeped in. He sat down on a high rock with his telescope, studied the terrain ahead, and finally saw what he had been looking for, the spiral of smoke that marked the soldiers' cook-fires.

He had found the end of the line, the pole setter's camp, and only then did he leave the high ground and drop down to the valley floor.

Some men would have been so elated that they would have abandoned their pot of water, figuring that soon plenty of water would be available, but Angevine hung onto the kettle. He had with him everything he had started with, even the ruined shoes because he didn't want to leave anything the Indians could find and trail him with.

He knew it would be well after dark before he reached the camp, but that did not matter now. He had made it back, he alone, afoot, injured, and he felt proud of this until he thought of Gore and the others, all dead, bare bones now.

Then he felt sorry that he had been denied the honor of dying with them because somehow, in the perverse nature of man, the victim of disaster was a hero and the survivor an oddity.

When he approached the camp, he made considerable noise and the guard shot at him. Angevine yelled and several other guards converged and fired their

44

rifles. He flung himself on the ground and remained there, yelling out his name until Lieutenant Bascomb arrived and put a stop to it.

Lanterns were fetched on the double and a dozen armed soldiers gathered, but they made no move past the perimeter of the camp until a civilian in buckskins pushed through, saying, "That ain't no Injun out there you damned fools." He boldly walked in Angevine's direction. "Sing out. I ain't got cat eyes, you know."

Angevine called and the civilian found him. "Easy there, little beaver," he said. Then he turned and yelled back, "All right, what you standin' there for? Come out and get him."

The soldiers came up with the lanterns and they looked at Angevine and he looked at them and at the civilian, a man in his forties, bearded and rather fierce in the eye. Lieutenant Bascomb arrived; he looked at Angevine and didn't recognize him.

"It's me, sir. Private Angevine."

"Angevine?" Bascomb said, as though he had just been confronted with an impossibility. "What are you doing here? What are those kettles? Have you lost your mind?"

The civilian said nothing but his face mirrored his disgust; he bent down and easily hauled Angevine to his feet, supporting him, taking him into the camp. "Come on there, little beaver," he kept saying. "It ain't but a small piece now. Jest put one foot 'head of t'other now. A few more there." He sighed when he lowered Angevine down by the fire. The others had followed him in and they stood around and looked at him as though he were some new species and they weren't sure whether he'd bite, bark, or crow.

The civilian acted as though he understood this completely and had gone through it twice daily and once on national holidays. He got a mug of coffee and some biscuits and soaked them and fed them to Loch Angevine. Now and then he'd let Angevine sip some of the coffee. Lieutenant Bascomb watched this for a time and then said, "Angevine, where are the others?"

"All dead, sir."

"Dead?" He sounded as though he were accusing him of lying.

The civilian looked at the lieutenant and said, "Let him catch his wind; he's come a far piece."

"I'll—report," Angevine said, feeling that this was the right thing, the brave thing to do. And it was what the lieutenant expected of him, a man who had no weaknesses, demanding that his men show none either. He looked at the lieutenant's resolute face, the calm, courageous eyes, and the noble chin, and suddenly he knew that he could not tell this man the exact truth, that they had been surprised and wiped out with hardly a shot being fired.

"They were Apaches, sir," Angevine said. "Took us by surprise, but the men fought valiantly, sir, beating them back, taking a dreadful toll, but they were too many for us, sir. Just too many."

The civilian nipped off a chaw of tobacco and worked his jaws on it and said nothing. The lieutenant waited.

46

"Well, sir, I went down. A knife in the back. When I came to, they were all dead. The sergeant and all of them and the Apaches had picked us clean of weapons and food and animals."

"How many Apaches were killed?" Bascomb asked.

Angevine shook his head, as though the actual count was hazy, but he knew he had to tell the lieutenant something, so he said, "I would say a dozen, sir."

He could see that this pleased the lieutenant as much as a promotion, and Bascomb said, "We'll send you back to the surgeon in the morning, Angevine. The major will want to question you. I suppose you can locate this place on a map?"

"Yes, sir. Sir, I'd like to remain in camp. I'll be all right in a few days."

"Nonsense," Bascomb said flatly. "Holly will take you back in the morning." He turned and went to his tent. The others stood around a minute or two longer, lost interest, and turned to their own blankets.

Holly, the civilian guide, took Angevine over to his own fire; it was a short distance away, separated from the main camp as though he could barely tolerate their company. Angevine was gently laid face down on a buffalo robe and Holly peeled off the underwear by soaking the blood-caked wound with water, softening it. He talked while he worked. "Hate to tell a man he's mistaken, beaver, but I'd lay you a prime plew again' a plug of trade tobackey that there warn't no dead Apaches." He inspected the wound carefully, grunting to himself. "Beaver, there's a broke off piece of knife

47

blade under the skin. Must have struck bone and broke clean off. I'll cut that out of there for ya if you want." He waited for Angevine to object, and when he didn't, Holly took out his greenriver knife, put the blade in the fire for a moment, then made one searing slash which made Angevine stiffen.

But he didn't cry out.

Holly took the chew of tobacco from his mouth, applied it to the wound and tightly bound Loch Angevine with strips of cloth. Then Holly said, "Feel some better now? Thought you would. You're a tough one, beaver. But you're a little mixed up about the Apaches, ain't you?"

Angevine turned his head and looked at Holly. "We didn't get more than four or five shots off. Never hit anything either."

"Didn't think you did," Holly said. "Apaches come like the wind, kill, and they're gone. If they thought you were alive, they'd have cooked your head over a low fire." He fell silent for a time. "I guess you done the right thing, tellin' the lootenant what he wanted to hear. These soldier fellas got a lot to learn, and I reckon they'll take a hell of a lickin' before they learn it. Apaches are always where you don't expect 'em, beaver. They hit quick and you've got to be set for 'em all the time." He put his hand on Angevine's shoulder. "You've got an edge now, beaver. You met the Apaches and lived through it, and there ain't many men who can claim that." He got up and stamped the kinks out of his legs. "Get some rest, beaver. Tomorrer

48

night you'll be in a bed in Santa Fe and an orderly will be waitin' on you hand and foot."

Lieutenant Bascomb sent a wagon and a detail back with Holly and when they arrived at Santa Fe, a detail from the contract surgeon met them and Angevine was taken into a building for medical treatment. He was bathed, shaved, his torn feet dressed, and his wound cared for. The surgeon did not seem to mind that Holly had applied his mountain man medicine, for he too believed that tobacco had the power to draw poison from a bad wound.

When it was completely understood how far Angevine had traveled, it became the talk of the post and a newspaper man came to the infirmary to interview him. A brush with the Apaches was news.

Angevine tried to make light of the whole thing, but the newspaper man had seen Lieutenant Bascomb's report and the lie was now a fact and no statement to the contrary would ever change it. By making them heroes, he had become one himself. He was very distressed over this, but the newspaperman immediately took his distress for acute modesty.

In three days, Angevine was up and walking about; his feet were giving him more trouble than his wound in the back, which was healing nicely. Both the infantry major and the cavalry major wanted to see him and an orderly walked with him to the building that served as the headquarters.

Both the majors smiled and he was asked to sit down and told to make himself comfortable.

The majors leaned their elbows on their desks and looked at him and the cavalry major said, "Now," as though the fun were over and business would begin. "My concern, Private Angevine, is about the cavalry detail that escorted the survey party. For the record, I want it down that they acquitted themselves nobly. Please relate the events to me."

He wanted to hear the lies too, but Angevine decided that it was more than that. He wanted to hear about the service, the honor of it, the dedication, so Angevine told him and the major kept nodding and saying, "Aaah," as though he were being deeply satisfied.

When Angevine was finished, the cavalry major looked at the infantry major and said, "I believe, Howard, that this may be one of the epic struggles of the frontier. I believe an immediate message to Washington is indicated."

The infantry major agreed. He looked at Loch Angevine. "Are your wounds bothering you, Private Angevine?"

"No, sir. I'm feeling better each day, sir. When can I return to duty?"

The major continued to study him. "Do you mean, return to the survey party?"

"Yes, sir."

His heroism obviously touched them deeply and for a moment they seemed almost too choked with pride to speak. "Who is your commanding officer?"

"Lieutenant Bascomb, sir."

"A splendid officer," the major declared. "I'll send

some dispatches with you. Have the quartermaster provide you with mules and your equipment. You may leave when the contract surgeon releases you from his care."

"Thank you, sir." Angevine stood, came to attention, and saluted.

The infantry major came around his desk and offered his hand. "I have noted your record, Angevine, and now that I've talked to you, I am of the opinion that you will go far in the service, distinguish yourself even further." He smiled. "You have the education and the courage. If you considered applying for a commission, I would consider most seriously the endorsement of it."

The interview was terminated and Angevine was glad to get outside. He walked slowly back to the barracks area, wondering again if it wouldn't have been much better to have told the terrible truth. Still the words wouldn't come out, not even when he had staggered into the base camp. It was not Gore's fault, or the fault of the others that they were slain before they could fight back, and in his mind that did not make them less brave than he knew them to be. Dying uselessly was heroic, wasn't it?

He thought it was.

In the days that followed, Angevine learned that the scene of the battle had been visited by Bascomb and his men, and because they found the bones of the brave men, the place was named Skeleton Ridge, a name that the newspaper people grabbed up because it had a scary excitement to it.

They knew what their readers wanted.

The fact that not one dead Indian was found seemed to alarm no one, for it was assumed that the surviving Apaches had taken their dead with them to be buried in some secret place to hide from all eyes the shame of their defeat.

And according to the newspapers, it *was* a defeat. Reporters somehow managed to work the number of Apache dead up to twenty-four, which made it about two to one, for there were only ten in the survey party, counting the cavalry escort.

Or perhaps the reporters got it as Angevine told it and the editor back east took license and juiced it up a bit. No one really cared, and if the military noticed the increase, they kept silent about it.

Angevine was known to everyone in Santa Fe, and people he didn't know wanted to pass the time of day with him. He responded in a pleasant, slightly withdrawn manner and never spoke of the Indian fight, which put him down as a right modest fellow, but one not to be tangled with lightly.

A photographer wanted him to pose for some pictures, and after some persuasion, Angevine agreed. The man had a studio set up in a vacant adobe and Angevine looked at some of the pictures he had taken of other Indian-fighters and scouts. They were a colorful lot, dressing in fringed buckskins and Indian beadwork and they carried big knives and fancy pistols and all wore their hair long.

He had gone unbarbered for months and intended to get a haircut, but he changed his mind after seeing the photographs. The photographer had a fringed jacket and a knife; he had Angevine put these on for the photographs, and afterward Angevine bought them for eleven dollars; he took to wearing them, except for inspections, and no one said anything about this irregularity of uniform.

Lieutenant Bascomb wired headquarters for a replacement noncom to lead the survey party, and the infantry major posted Loch Angevine's name on the board, promoted to corporal. This happened the day before Angevine made ready to leave for the end of line camp; the same day he bought a broad-brimmed western hat and a pair of bone handles for his .44 Remington.

The sutler's wife sewed the corporal's hooks on his sleeves.

When he left the town, he was riding one mule and leading another heavily loaded, and although the weather was hot, he wore the fringed jacket and kept the hat pulled low over his eyes. People stood on the walks and under the porches and watched him ride out, and when he passed the camp of the wagon travelers, he heard one man say, "Who's that feller?" and another answered, "That's Angevine, the Injun-fighter." Respect and admiration immediately came into the other man's eyes and he waved, taking his pipe out of his mouth when he did so.

That night Angevine saw the fires of a wagon party

that had left Santa Fe the day before. He rode right into their camp without being challenged and he thought that this was a foolish thing that might get them killed. They were movers, mostly, families with wives and children and everything they owned, traveling southwest toward Silver City and then on west, following the Gila River into Arizona.

His arrival in the camp caused somewhat of a stir, for several of the men recognized him and the word got around that Angevine, the Indian-fighter, was in the camp.

He was taken to a cook-fire and fed; the man's name was Wrigley and he was leading the train. The men gathered around while Angevine ate, and the women and children stayed back a ways and watched too.

Finally Angevine said, "If I was you, I'd post a strong guard." Then, remembering the killing and eating of the mule, he added, "Apaches like mule meat. They could hit your herd before you knew it."

His tone had been conversational, and the manner of his suggestion almost shy, as though he were reluctant to speak, to intrude his opinion on older men. Yet they reacted as though Gospel had been read to those eager to be saved. Wrigley had no trouble getting ten armed men for guard duty and within minutes these men were at their posts.

He insisted that Angevine have more coffee, and one of the women had some leftover pastry and this was brought to him on a tin plate. Wrigley said, "We're farm folks and this is strange country. We want to get through and we'll leave the Injuns alone if they do the same to us. Any help you might give—"

Angevine sat there and thought about the smoke he had seen two days before they had been hit; it was obvious now that the Apaches signaled each other that way and organized their raiding parties. Gore had paid no mind to the smoke, but Angevine knew now that it was important.

And he remembered how quiet the land had been that evening; nothing had stirred, no birds or animals.

He raised his eyes and looked at them; they seemed to be waiting with held breath, waiting for wisdom to pour forth from him. So he said, "Keep an eye to the high, far promontories. Look for smoke. They call to each other that way. Be alert if the land turns quiet. They're about then and fixing to strike."

They nodded and murmured their thanks and one woman said, "God bless you, Injun-fighter," and he felt very embarrassed but managed not to show it. His silence was taken for thoughtfulness and his casual manner for stoicism; they read into his words and actions what they wanted most to hear and see and feel, and he was totally helpless to change that.

He was given a place by the fire to sleep and no one disturbed him.

Even the changing of the guard was done quietly.

4

Lieutenant Bascomb was in charge of the advance survey party, a duty he did not relish because he preferred the greater comfort of the main wire-stringing camp, and there he had a better chance of controlling all facets of the operation.

When Corporal Angevine arrived at the advance camp, Bascomb seemed almost overjoyed to see him; he immediately got out his map case and discussed the route with Angevine. They were about one hundred miles east of Silver City and more than a hundred and seventy miles ahead of the pole crew, a distance that irritated Bascomb because he wanted to get back there and jog them into increased activity.

Yet he couldn't leave the advance camp because they had no surveyor to put in charge.

Loch Angevine solved that very nicely.

"I have six men in the crew, three cavalry soldiers, and Holly as guide," Bascomb said, folding his maps. "Those damned fools at base camp have been sitting on their hands and I mean to kick a few asses when I get back there. So I'm putting you in charge here, corporal. Remain four or five days and get your equipment in shape. We'll catch up with the schedule and you push on to Silver City. We've got to have that wire strung and the line open and operating by the 30th of June."

He spoke in a tone Angevine had heard him use only

56

with sergeants and other officers, a straight out, man-to-man and damn-the-rank kind of tone. He closed his map case and looked steadily at Loch Angevine. "I'm going to count on you because I know I can."

"Yes, sir."

"We've had no Indian trouble. Probably won't after the drubbing you gave them. Lick them good once and they'll learn respect for the army. Right?"

"Yes, sir."

Bascomb immediately called the cavalry corporal over and told him that he was leaving and that Angevine was in charge. With that he gathered his gear, got his horse, and rode north, trailing a good plume of dust.

The cavalry corporal wasn't very happy at having a newly made corporal outrank him, but he knew better than to make anything of it. Angevine looked over the camp; the small tents were pitched and a spring was nearby, higher up in a clutter of rocks. He thought that they were camped too much in the open, but then he figured that if there was any real danger, Holly would have said something about it, so he kept his mouth shut.

Holly came in—he'd been on a meat-hunting foray—and he gave a small deer to the soldier who had been detailed to the cooking. When he saw Angevine, he smiled and shook hands.

"You're lookin' some better, little beaver."

"Feel better," Angevine said. "The lieutenant went back and left me in charge."

"Waugh! Maybe we can get out of here then," Holly said. "Been two days here and I don't like lingerin' in one spot."

Angevine shook his head and relayed the lieutenant's orders. Holly thought about this, rubbing his whiskered chin. Then he said, "Well, he didn't say we couldn't move from this gully, did he? Hell of a place. We ought to be somewhere above the spring in the rocks." He looked up and pointed. "Was there enough room at the spring, I'd say to camp there, but they ain't. Nearest place is a pocket 'bout fifty yards to the right and up a piece." He swung his arm to indicate the direction.

"We'll move," Angevine said and gave the order.

There were several reasons why it was not instantly obeyed: he was a new corporal and hadn't proven himself; they didn't know him very well, so he wasn't a friend; and moving would take work and they wanted to take the easiest way out.

Then he said the magic words: "I got caught once in this kind of a camp and I'm not going to do it again. Who'll survive this one?" He looked from man to man, and by the time he had stared at each of them, they were ready to move.

Holly selected the site; it was fairly well protected and backed against a sheer wall a hundred feet high. A narrow path led to the spring which was below them and the path was open. The spring itself was hardly more than a six-foot-square gouge in the rock, fed by some hidden seep. It was not big enough for a camp

and it was not a good place to defend, for it was surrounded only by a modest pile of rocks; from the other
side of the canyon, at the rim, a good rifleman used to
long shots could make life difficult for anyone
crouched down at the spring.

That evening, along about dusk, Angevine got out
his telescope and made a careful study of the far
mountain rises, and when he found smoke to the north
and east, he called Holly for an opinion.

The guide had a look, then said, "Well, I guess
they're either after Bascomb or us."

"Us," Angevine said. "We've got mules."

Holly grunted and studied the smoke through the
glass until the light failed, then he handed the glass
back and Angevine put it away.

"Was I to offer an opinion," he said, "I'd do all I
could to fortify this place. I'd pile rocks up for a good
bulwark to protect the mules and come daylight I'd
make up a detail to go to that spring and fetch up five-
six days' supply of water." He squinted at the far
mountains. "Day after tomorrer we can expect company."

"I don't mean to be surprised like I was the last
time," Angevine said.

He set everyone to work right after the evening meal
and they worked most of the night because there was
a good moon and enough light. When dawn arrived,
they had all the loose rock picked up and piled around
their camp.

It was Holly's opinion that the Apaches couldn't

gather in time to attack, so he and Angevine and two others went to the spring with the canvas water bags and canteens and filled them up.

The sky was just flushing gray and lightening rapidly in the east. They filled the bags and one man loaded himself with them and took them back, walking up the narrow, steep slope to the camp.

Holly laid his .44 Henry repeater and canvas cartridge belt down in order to bend way down to dip in his canteen, for in filling the water bags, they had lowered the level in the hole considerably. The cavalry soldier stood behind Holly and for some reason he took out his Remington pistol and checked the loads in it, half cocking it and spinning the cylinder in a series of dry clicks.

Angevine, who had yet to fill his canteen, knelt on the other side of the water hole and when he heard the cylinder spin, he looked up and while he watched, a rifle sound fractured the silence and the cavalry soldier grabbed his upper arm, spun around, and dropped the pistol.

The Apaches swooped down upon them like a wave dashing against a forlorn beach, rushing across the narrow canyon and bolting into the rocks in order to climb to the water hole.

"I'm gettin' the hell outa here!" Holly said and grabbed his canteen and ran up the trail toward the camp. The Apaches fired a ragged volley at him and bullets whipped around him and sang off the rocks and by some miracle he was not hit at all. The last

Angevine saw of him was his headlong dive to the cover of the barricade.

There was no time to be afraid and Angevine, sensitive to the attack that had wounded him, sighted carefully with his Remington, squeezed one off, and shot one of the Apaches flush in the face. The Indian went down like a chucked stone and suddenly they stopped shooting at the barricaded camp and turned their attack again to the water hole.

The cavalry soldier, wounded in the fleshy part of his upper arm, took one look at the Apaches making it up through the rocks and dashed up the trail toward the camp. He ran in a crouch, his boots churning dirt and pebbles and the Apaches tried to cut him down, but Loch Angevine kept firing his pistol, hitting another and driving the others down into the rocky cover.

The cavalry soldier made it; hands pulled him over and suddenly the shooting stopped; the soldiers were waiting for an attack and the Apaches—who never had enough cartridges—were saving their ammunition.

Holly yelled, "Come on 'er, beaver! Run and we'll cover ya!"

This was sound advice, given by a man Angevine acknowledged as knowing of Indian ways, but he looked at the narrow, steep trail right out there in the open, bathed now in the first morning sunlight, and he knew that he just didn't have the nerve to get up and run.

It was a terrible feeling to have, and he felt as though he had been stripped naked in public, every blemish, every secret exposed.

"Come on 'er, beaver!" Holly yelled again.

Angevine didn't answer him. There was nothing to say. He couldn't tell them that he preferred to stay where he was because a blind idiot could see that the water hole didn't offer enough protection. Even crawling he would be partially exposed, especially when the Apaches started shooting from the other wall of the canyon.

He knew that he wasn't going to budge, to break for the trail, and once he knew that, he decided to make a fight of it. The Apaches wanted the water hole; they needed the water. But he was squatting there, an armed man, denying them the use of it.

For how long was a question that he didn't bother to debate.

He had one shot left in his pistol. Then he saw the other Remington that the cavalry soldier had dropped and he reached for it, hefted it, and felt a lot better. His own single-shot carbine lay to one side and he looked at it, then saw Holly's repeater and cartridge belt. For a moment he stared, like some small boy staggered by the presents under the Christmas tree.

He laid aside the cavalryman's pistol, still cocked. Then he picked up the rifle, worked the lever and fed a .44 rimfire into the chamber. With a fury of yelling, the Apaches rushed the water hole, leaving their cover; the farthest was no more than forty yards away now.

The soldiers behind the barricade began to fire, but it was Angevine who broke their backs. Rising to his knees, upper body completely exposed, he fired the Henry as fast as he could work the lever, laying down a field of fire that sent two of the attackers rolling lifeless down to the canyon floor and the others ducking to cover.

Holly let out a ringing war whoop and the firing died off and a deep, filling silence settled over the mountains. Angevine reloaded the Henry—he had fired fourteen times—and when that was done, he crushed paper cartridges into his Remington and capped the nipples.

He laid this revolver beside the cavalryman's and bellied down to wait.

An hour passed and the sun climbed and the heat built and no one stirred. Angevine felt like a man who had taken a lot of photographs and was now faced with the difficult task of sorting them out. He sorted his fragmented impressions and decided that there were about fifteen Apaches in this war party. He had killed three himself because he had seen them fall, and if any were wounded, he didn't count them.

Only the dead ones.

He looked toward the camp. They wouldn't be much help to him because they were too high, and a curve in the trail and an outcropping of rock prevented any of them from actually pouring fire down onto the perimeter of the spring.

The Apaches knew this and that was why they

wanted to work close in. Within ten yards of the spring they would be out of the line of fire from the barricade and they could rush the rest of the way, cut him down and get the water they needed.

It was a helpless feeling, to be too afraid to leave, and yet afraid to stay; he knew that he would be killed making a run up the trail, and for certain he would be killed if he stayed at the spring.

Several times he thought he had gathered the courage to run for it, but each time it deserted him and left him sweating and shaken. Then two Apaches, proving their courage, leaped up and began climbing, screaming at the top of their lungs.

Angevine snatched up the Henry rifle and shot one through the throat and saw him fall, but the other one came on and he fired too quickly, hitting the Indian in the thigh.

The Apache was at the edge of the water hole and he leaped across, but landed on his wounded leg and fell and the knife he swung missed Angevine and gave him a chance to turn and back out of the way. He fired the rifle from the hip and the bullet caught the Apache in the breast, making a deep pucker that immediately began to gush blood.

He looked into the Apache's eyes; there was life still there, and hate, and an animal will to kill, and he shot again, more accurately this time, and the Indian fell dead.

Because the dead Indian crowded the water hole, Loch Angevine tugged and pushed and finally rolled him on down among the rocks where he bounced and flung about a bit and then came to rest against a boulder.

There was a cheering from the camp and he wondered what the damned fools were yelling about and hated them for not coming out and getting him out of his impossible situation.

The Apaches were completely silent, motionless behind their cover now, and several hours dragged by. The sun was a torch and he kept soaking his handkerchief and bathing his head and face and waiting for them to attack again.

He was surprised at his own patience, his own calm frame of mind, and he tried to understand this. He held out his hand and looked at it: it was steady with no trembling of the fingers. In fact, he felt so calm that he would have lighted a cigar had he been a smoking man. He supposed that this was a human trait, to adjust to changes, no matter how unpleasant, and his fear had been so strong that he had learned to ignore it.

Or at least he felt he had settled into it.

He looked up the trail and decided that he could run up that damned thing any time he felt like it, but right now he didn't feel like it. He was defending the water hole, and he wasn't doing too bad a job of it, and by God he was going to stay there too.

His powder flask was nearby and he began to get an idea. The paper cartridges were waxed and soaked in saltpeter so that they burned cleanly, so he stripped off three and wound the paper tightly into a fuse about three inches long. Then he opened his powder flask, stuck one end in, but pulled it out immediately, realizing that the spring-loaded measure would slice it off. He then unscrewed the cap, pushed the fuse into the powder, and sealed the end with mud.

By his estimation, that fuse was good for about thirty seconds, which meant he had to light it and throw it immediately. The chances that it would blow up in his face were considerable, but he was compelled to go ahead with this.

With the bomb made and the match ready, Angevine selected his target, a jumble of rocks fifteen yards down the slope that hid several Apaches. He lit the fuse, hauled back, and arced it over, watching it curve up and down, and it seemed to explode an instant before it hit.

He was rewarded with a lot of surprised yelling and two of the Apaches turned and bolted down the rocky slope toward the canyon floor, but six leaped to their feet and charged.

Angevine snatched up the pair of pistols and stood erect, firing as fast as he could cock and pull the triggers. He saw one Apache fold in the middle and fall and then there was so much powder smoke between him and the Indians that he couldn't see whether he had hit anything or not.

But he emptied the pistols, all twelve rounds, and bellied down, the Henry once again in his hands.

Then the sudden noise died away completely, the

powder smoke dissipated, and he was still alone at the water hole. For a moment he rested and stilled the wild beating of his heart. There was a rent in the sleeve of his buckskin jacket and a slash on the brim of his hat and for a moment he couldn't figure out how that had happened. Then he realized that bullets had done that and this made him very nervous and a little sick at his stomach.

He bathed his head and face and felt better and rested, wishing that he had something to eat.

The waiting was bad, but the fighting was worse, so he used the last of his paper cartridges to load the pistols and counted the shells remaining in Holly's belt— sixteen. Enough for another reloading after he had emptied the magazine.

After that he guessed he'd grab the damned thing by the barrel and beat the brains out of the first Apache who jumped over the rim.

The sun was beginning to set when he got the notion that the Apaches were not going to try again, and he raised up and had a little look out there to see what was going on. The dead ones lay where they had fallen, but there was some activity farther down, and it looked like they were trying to pull one behind some cover. Sighting over the rifle barrel, Angevine could see hands tugging, and he took care and put a bullet through someone's wrist.

That brought a howl, but it was pain and rage, and the battle cry wasn't about to be taken up. Suddenly there was a mad bolting down the slope, the Apaches rushing, leaping from rock to rock, dodging the sudden fusilade from the barricade.

There was no use in firing, so Angevine lowered his rifle and stood up to ease the horrible cramps in his legs. The Apaches were gone and the shooting quit and then Holly and the soldiers boiled out from behind the barricade and came running down the slope to the spring.

Holly jumped up and down and danced and pounded his moccasins in the dirt and raised a frightful cloud of dust. "I doggies, little beaver, if'n you don't take the hide off a mule!" He thumped Angevine on the back and roughed him up in an excited, good-natured way. "Now if you ain't a whole team and a dog under the wagon! If'n it warn't enough to kill 'em, you had to go an' roll 'em down the mountain side! That's the beat of anythin' I 'er seen!"

The soldiers watched him dance and whoop and finally he stopped and picked up his rifle. "She shoots fair to good, don't she, beaver?"

"You left in a hurry," Angevine said. "Forgot it more than likely, huh?"

Holly sobered. "Beaver, I got a rule and I never break it: Where Apaches is, I ain't." He winked. "Doggone fool, when I seen you was set on defendin' the water hole, I was sorry I'd left." He waved his hand to include the others. "By golly, if'n the corporal hadn't done some quick thinkin,' some of you'd be dead now. Them Apaches needed water. Had they got their bags full, they'd have hung around three, maybe four days,

68

snipin' at us, cuttin' us down one at a time." He mauled Angevine on the back and nearly drove him flat. "But, beaver, you done held the fort. By golly if you didn't. You put the bad medicine on them Apaches. Yes sir, that there bomb plumb scared the hell out of 'em!"

"They might be back," Angevine said seriously.

"Naaaaw, they won't be back," Holly said. "They've been whupped, boy! Come on, let's go take a look at them dead Apaches. Known men who've lived many a year and never seen one."

Angevine didn't want to go; the killing was bad enough, but Holly was in a gleeful mood and so were the others, and he supposed it had been this way with the pagan hordes in Europe, flushed with battle, hard to hold down, with rape and pillage as their only release.

He went down the slope with them and there were seven dead Apaches, grotesque and bloody and dirty and most unpleasant to look at. Holly said, "What you gonna do, corporal? You leave 'em here and the blow-flies'll be after 'em tomorrow. Next day they'll be bloated and stink so bad you can't stand it."

Angevine stood there, gravely considering what he should do, pushed strongly by instinct and training to provide a Christian burial, although the Apaches wouldn't understand it or appreciate it. He said, "Holly, can we make Silver City by tomorrow afternoon if we travel all night?"

"Could," Holly said. "What for?" Then his expression brightened. "Why shore, beaver! Let's give them see-villyans a look at dead Injuns fer a change! Besides, we can dump 'em off at the undertaker."

"That was my real motive," Angevine said.

"Shore it was," Holly said, winking and nudging Angevine. "I'll go fetch a couple of mules."

"You won't be going," Angevine said. "I'll go and take two of the cavalrymen along. You'll stay here with the others like the lieutenant said."

"Aaaawshit! Then fetch me back a bottle of lightnin'."

"I'll do that," Angevine said. "Get some blankets to cover the Apaches with. I'd like to leave in an hour. We'll travel out the night. There'll be a moon and I can tell direction by the stars."

"Ain't that somethin'?" Holly said and went giggling and chuckling up the slope to the camp.

Two cavalrymen volunteered to make the all night ride with Angevine and the mules were loaded, the Apaches securely tied on. After the horses got over their fear of the blood smell, they settled down and made a proper march of it.

Angevine stuck close to the cavalry march rules, dismounting for a time out of each hour to walk the horses, and because of this they covered a lot of miles without killing the horses. Rest was what they could take in the saddle, with only the briefest pauses for housekeeping and watering the horses.

Silver City was crouched in mountains whose flanks already bore the scars of greedy men burrowing for ore. The arrival of the army with the dead Apaches caused as much excitement as a five-alarm fire, and the newspaper editor collared one of the cavalrymen for the full story of it.

Angevine went to the express office and wrote a message, to be taken by stage to Santa Fe; Lieutenant Bascomb would want to know the details as quickly as possible, and Angevine couched the events in the briefest terms and listed the wounded army men and the number of dead Indians.

When he reached the start, men followed him down the walk and stopped when he stopped and went into the stores he stepped into and followed him back onto the street. He remembered his promise to Holly and entered one of the numerous saloons and approached the bar. An aisle opened for him and men stepped back and gave him a clear spot.

He ordered a bottle of whiskey and when he went to pay for it, money appeared as though by magic and he found that he could spend nothing. He was offered drinks and refused them and because he was what he was, no one was offended at all.

He rested for several hours in the stable, then got the two cavalrymen and the horses and mules and started back. People watched him go and talked about him long after he left town.

The undertaker put the Apaches on display until the odor became so offensive that he had to bury them, and he did this with great reluctance for at fifty cents a head, he had a gold mine on his hands.

But like everything else, it petered out.

5

What is a smile to one man is a sneer to another, and opinion varies like the accuracy of a cheap pocket watch. As far as Loch Angevine was concerned, Holly was his best friend, and best friends can do no wrong.

While some of the survey detail considered Holly's hasty retreat from the water hole as just plain being scared out of his pants, Loch Angevine looked upon it as a bit of wisdom, and the fact that he hadn't followed Holly was because he had lacked Holly's courage in running the gauntlet of fire.

Others figured that Holly, if cornered fifteen minutes after something happened, would likely tell you the straight of it, but given a few days to think it over, the story would likely be embellished a bit, and a couple of months later it would pretty much be a pack of lies.

Angevine thought this grossly unfair and he listened to Holly's stirring tales of adventure very carefully and he learned a lot. He felt that it was not Holly's fault that he became embroiled in adventures so fantastic that it stretched the imagination to accept them. Holly, by his own admission, was a personal friend of Kit Carson and Hugh Glass and a lot of the other mountain men. Holly could, he confessed, speak fluently the Crow tongue, and Blackfoot, and had mastered the sign language of all the Plains Indians by the time he was thirteen.

Holly time and time again proved to Angevine his bigness by forgiving others for taking credit for the things he had done, the discoveries he had made. At fourteen, long before Jim Bridger made his northward trek, Holly had searched out the headwaters of the Missouri and made friends with the terrible Blackfeet. And if it hadn't been for Holly, future explorations in that area would have met with extermination, for it was his relationship with the Blackfeet that gave the white man the foothold he needed to cheat and rob them blind and eventually drive them out.

As the survey party moved on toward Silver City, Angevine spent the evenings in camp with Holly, talking with him, listening to him, and learning vast stores of Indian lore. Holly knew the flight of every bird, the habit of every animal, and he had a deep and thorough knowledge of the Indians—their customs, habits, and thinking. There was not a dance or religious ceremony that Holly did not understand, and upon several occasions he had been adviser to Crow medicine men.

When they reached Silver City, the survey party made camp on the west edge of the town to wait there for orders from Lieutenant Bascomb. Angevine had the tents pitched in neat rows and a picket line for the horses set up and he posted one man on guard and allowed two at a time liberty in town. All this made the soldiers grumbly, for they felt that they ought to be able to come and go as they pleased.

Angevine always went into town with Holly; he felt

no kinship at all to the others. In town, Angevine went to a gunsmith and bought a .44 Henry repeater, the same as Holly's, and he bought two bandoliers of cartridges and a couple of spare boxes. Wherever he went, he carried the rifle and he became a familiar figure in his buckskin coat and hat with the bullet tear in the brim.

It pleased Angevine that Holly wanted to go along with him into town and he was proud to be with the scout, even though he disliked Holly's drinking so much. Yet he knew better than to try to correct Holly or even say anything about it.

When Angevine got tired of it, he'd tell Holly he was tired and go on back to camp. Sometimes Holly wouldn't come back until dawn, and then he'd be roaring drunk and wake everyone.

Holly had long ago spent all his money, yet he always seemed to be able to scare up enough to get drunk. Angevine didn't understand this, but he supposed Holly had ways that he did not share with any man.

Unfortunately Angevine never stayed long enough in the saloons to find out, for Holly always had a ready audience who kept his glass filled.

It was worth the price of a drink to hear him talk.

And he had a new subject: Corporal Loch Angevine.

Holly would stand at the bar, weaving slightly, spouting forth.

". . . ne'er seen the beat of him . . . no, sir, never did . . . reads 'Pache smoke . . . yeah, he does . . . speaks their language like his own . . . you should heard him at the spring . . . jabberin' back'n forth with 'em . . . cussin' 'em out, I guess . . . raised with 'em, you know . . . yeah . . . ne'er know it to look at him . . . educated fella and all . . . good family too . . . jined up on account of a woman . . . beautiful thing . . . weddin' all set an' ever'thin' . . ."

The drinks kept coming.

". . . dead shot, I tell you . . . never seen such shootin', an' I've seen the best . . . you seen that gash in his hat and in his coat? . . . he stood up thar in full view when they charged . . . yellin', 'Take that, you red-hide varmints!' . . . 'course he was talkin' 'Pache but I know a mite of it m'self and got the gist right off . . . then cool as you please he fired twice and dropped two in their tracks . . ."

He would look around because his glass was empty; he was a human music box that operated on whisky instead of nickels.

". . . he survived that fight on Skeleton Ridge, y'know . . . walked the hull way back, bullet and knife and arrer holes in him . . . he's a real tough one . . . kill any man who'd cross him, likely . . . take care myself to keep on the good side o' him . . . yessiree, I don't cross him at all . . . them soldiers jump when he talks too . . ."

Night after night Holly held up the various bars in town while Angevine slept peacefully at his camp. And in the daytime, while Holly slept off the residue of his wild night, Angevine would go into town to replenish supplies and to check at the stage office for any communication from Lieutenant Bascomb.

Angevine was impressed with the courtesy these rough people accorded him; even the burliest miners and the well-known toughs and gunslingers took care to walk gently around him, and when he happened to speak to one, the answer was always carefully phrased so as not to offend.

To his surprise, he found Wrigley's wagon party camped on the other side of town; they had arrived while the dead Apaches were on exhibit and it had so frightened them that they had halted their journey until some appeal could be made to the military for some escort on to Tucson.

Angevine visited their camp and created a great deal of excitement, which hadn't been his intention at all. He had merely wanted to renew his brief acquaintance with Wrigley and some of the others, and perhaps cadge a meal in the hope that one of the women had prepared bread or a pie.

Wrigley insisted that a table be set up for Angevine, and a cloth spread and food from all over the camp was gathered to make sure he had the best they had to offer. The more he protested at this fuss, the more determined they became to excel.

He had a fine stew and some pieces of ham and fresh bread and boiled potatoes and a piece of mince pie. Wrigley and a few other leaders sat with him, and when he was through eating, they came to the matter that was uppermost in their minds—getting on to Tucson.

76

"We would leave if we had someone to guide us through Apache Pass," Wrigley said.

One man said, "The Mexicans call it, *Puerto del Dado,* the doorway of the dice. And I guess it's worth a man's life to go through there."

"But others have done it," Wrigley said, "and we'll do it, with God's help and yours, Injun-fighter."

"I'm a soldier," Angevine said. "I couldn't leave my post or my duty." He smiled. "Besides, you're overestimating my ability, sir."

This modesty made them smile and chuckle, for they all knew the truth about him, how he knew Apaches and their ways. Wrigley said, "I'm going to talk to your officer; I've heard talk around the town that they should be here in a few days or a week. If he gives permission for the army to escort us, will you be the guide?"

"Well, if I'm ordered, I'll go," Angevine said, and then opened his mouth to say that Holly was really the one qualified.

But they cut in on him with their thanks and their hand shaking and sincere gratitude, and he was so touched by it that he could not bear to sweep away their renewed hope.

So he said his goodbyes and returned to his own camp and didn't think much would come of Wrigley's appeal, for the army had their own work, and a trip to Tucson and back would take at least thirty days. The wagons would move slowly and Tucson was nearly two hundred and fifty miles from Silver City.

Lieutenant Bascomb arrived with the cavalry major and twenty-six men in the escort, and according to the immediate gossip, the pole setters and wire stringing crew was less than eight miles behind.

The cavalry major was impressed with the orderly condition of the survey camp and ordered his troopers to use the same site. The command tent was pitched at the head of the company street and then Corporal Angevine was summoned. The major was there and Lieutenant Bascomb was there and they all exchanged salutes. Then the major and the lieutenant smiled and offered Angevine a drink and a cigar and a chair, in that order.

The major flounced his mustache and rocked back and forth on his heels and beamed. "Corporal, when Lieutenant Bascomb showed me your report, I was delighted. Simply delighted. We will show these bloody devils who is in charge, won't we?"

"Yes, sir."

"You may be pleased to know," the major said, "that the general has authorized me to raise you to sergeant in spite of your brief length of time in service. The army is not immune to our talented men, Angevine."

"Thank you, major. I only tried to do my best."

"Of course, of course." He hid momentarily behind the quickly puffed cloud of cigar smoke. Then he waved it away like a man brushing steam from a window so he could peer out. "Very good thinking, bringing those dead Apaches here, sergeant. Good to let these civilians know that the army is not only capable but on the job, eh?"

"Yes, sir. But I really just wanted to get them buried, sir."

"What's that?" He stared, then laughed. "Having your little joke, eh, sergeant? All right, you've earned the right to it." Then his manner turned very serious. "The lieutenant and I hardly got a chance to cut the dust from our throats before a man named Wrigley pounced on us. Wants an escort through Apache Pass. Wants you to lead them and a cavalry escort." He frowned and puffed some more on his cigar. "My first impression was to tell him to go to the devil, but civilians vote, sergeant. They vote and elect congressmen and senators who decide whether or not the army is going to have money. We don't travel on our stomachs, regardless of what's been said." Then he chuckled and looked quickly at Bascomb, who chuckled also. Angevine smiled because he was a sergeant.

"So after due consideration," the major said, "I think I'll provide an escort, sergeant. We have maps of that area and you've already shown me that you can handle the Indians, so I think it would be wise to take them through. After all, a letter of praise from a voter to his congressman is better than one of criticism. Right?"

"Yes, sir."

The interview was terminated and Angevine stepped outside and replaced his hat. As he started to walk away, Bascomb came out and hailed him and they walked on a bit and then stopped in the shade of a grove.

Bascomb stood very straight and his expression was stiff. "The major is very pleased with you, sergeant. I consider that important because he's cavalry and is inclined to be critical. Your wounds no longer bother you?"

"No, sir, and thank you for asking." He smiled. "But I am sorry I'm not serving with you, sir. I'd like to, if possible, so that I can learn from you . . . sir."

Bascomb peered down his nose, his manner suspicious; he was an officer and because of this distinction he suspected the motives of all enlisted men. "It'll go hard with you if you're playing a game with me, Angevine."

"I was most serious, sir. I'd like to learn how to conduct myself as you do, sir."

"And exactly how is that, Angevine?"

"With dignity, sir. You're a very positive man, sir."

For once the officer seemed at a loss for words. Finally he said, "Enough of this nonsense, sergeant. You have your place and your duty and I have mine, and that's all there is to it." He wheeled and stalked off, his back as stiff as a pick handle, whether with pride or embarrassment it was hard to tell.

Once the decision to escort the wagon party through had been made, preparation to leave got under way, with Sergeant Angevine in charge. With his meager knowledge of Indians and fighting in general, and a

80

large caution backed by an enormous doubt of his ability pushing him, he insisted that the men and boys of the wagon party be heavily armed, and because he did not trust their marksmanship, he declared that each would be armed with a double-barreled shotgun.

The gunsmith sold out his stock and worked day and night for three days, converting older shotguns into the breech-loaders. Angevine, in considering fire-power, knew that the single-shot rifles were a handicap: they took too long to load. But the shotguns, with their brass cartridge cases, were faster to load, surer to fire, and each contained two shots.

Heavy buckshot at fifty yards was better than a bullet for cutting a man down; he felt this was so because most all the guards on the stages used shotguns, and these men knew what they were doing.

The cavalry detail was picked by the major and put in command of a sergeant, who had orders to stay with the train and to guard it until it reached Tucson, then return promptly. This maneuver, Angevine thought, was cleverly done, for it left the cavalry sergeant in command of his men, and Angevine in command of the train without a conflict of who was boss of what.

Holly, now that official eyes were on him, remained clear of the saloons and sobered up and became his old, friendly, helpful self again. And because the end of wire would remain in Silver City for a time, he was free to go along with the wagon party, a thing that made Loch Angevine feel downright relieved.

The actual departure caused a great deal of excitement in the town. Finally they drew clear of it and pushed on westward toward the Chiricahua Mountains, making an easy twelve miles a day without killing mules or shaking the wagons to pieces.

They traveled through mountainous country and bare, brush-dotted ridges that stuck up like bare bones. Often men would have to move ahead of the wagons to move stones from the trail.

Angevine, once he knew that he would be leading the train, had spent many hours poring over the maps, memorizing prominent landmarks and studying the topography with a surveyor's natural instinct for rise and fall.

The pass and the spring there was located some thirty-five miles from what eventually became the Arizona-New Mexico border and one hundred and twenty miles east of their destination, Tucson.

And because he worried over his responsibility, Angevine kept to himself at the night camps and no one bothered him because they took this to be the natural way of a man who had once lived as savagely as the Indians they now wished to avoid.

Holly was his companion, and the civilians understood this, these two wolves seeking their own company.

But Holly wasn't much help although by his own declaration he had been the discoverer of the pass. When Angevine questioned him closely, Holly's memory failed him and he kept saying that as they got farther along it would all come back.

Angevine couldn't blame him. He felt sorry for Holly because it was the heavy drinking that had fogged his mind and made him fuzzy-headed. He knew that once Holly got farther along the trail, it *would* come back to him, and because he believed that, he didn't worry.

On the sixth day they were making the eastern approach, and as the wagons teetered and rattled up the canyon, the walls began to squeeze and narrow until there was not room for three wagons to drive abreast.

The canyon walls were too sheer, too rough for the cavalry to put outriders on station, for the horses couldn't climb them and the troopers had no intention of dismounting.

The canyon was dotted with trees; walnut and mulberry and clumps of mesquite and low hanging branches caught and tore the wagon covers until finally they stopped to have these and the bows removed.

The spring, according to Angevine's maps, was barely a half mile away and he kept the wagons going and the men riding with the shotguns ready, and the cavalry kept searching the tops of the canyon, but there was no sign of Apaches.

At the summit, they started down suddenly, for the pass opened to a valley with a dense clump of trees marking the location of the spring. Keeping the wagons moving—they all wanted to stop and sigh with relief—Angevine took his telescope and studied the mountains beyond, searching the high ground for smoke but seeing none.

Yet he knew that this didn't mean there weren't any Indians about.

When they reached the spring, he insisted that the wagons be drawn up tightly to form a defense, and this was met with some objection because they felt safe now with trees and water about. He marveled that simple, familiar objects like trees and water could lull a man into acting carelessly.

He saw that a heavy guard was posted and no one was allowed to go after water or to water stock unless guarded by two men. A lot of the movers thought this was pure military hogwash—all right for the army which didn't have much else to do, but a damned bother to men intent on getting down the trail.

But he was the Indian-fighter and they looked at him and remembered and they looked at his Henry rifle and then did what he wanted. The women didn't like to be penned up in the wagon compound and the children wanted to run and play, but the guards kept turning them back and there was a lot of grumbling about this.

None of it did any good.

Angevine and Holly were scouting the spring and Holly found tracks. He spat tobacco and said, "'Paches."

"How can you tell?" Angevine asked, eager to learn.

Holly stared at him a moment. "Hell, beaver, I see tracks, don't I? Who the hell lives in these hills? So they're 'Pache." He shook his head as though boggled by such stupidity; it had been very evident to him. "You jest got to think more, beaver. Danged if'n I can hang 'round forever and take care of you."

With this said, he returned to the camp, and Angevine trailed him, a few paces behind.

The men didn't like to stand guard half the night, but they did it, and Angevine half expected the Apaches to hit them at dawn, but the sun came up and the birds twittered and fluttered about in the trees and there were no Indians.

Holly's opinion was that the movers had displayed such an alertness and number of arms that the Indians wouldn't risk attack. The movers all looked at Angevine to see what the Indian-fighter thought of this, and when he nodded, that cinched it in their minds.

They remained at the spring another day and night, then moved on, the animals refreshed and the washing done and the spring good and muddied, which was bound to make the Apaches happy, and Angevine insisted that the strong guard be kept at each camp and that every man ride alert and ready to fight.

This was met with a gale of complaint and he marveled at the contrary nature of man, who would beg for expert advice, then object to it when it didn't suit him.

The trip and constant worry took a toll on his nervous system and finally when one man said the wrong thing at the wrong time, Angevine lost his temper, swung the butt of his Henry rifle and put the man flat on the ground, with one blow while his wife and children stared in horror.

And seeing the man stretched out, a bloody cut on his head where the metal bloodplate had struck him, Angevine was filled with self-loathing and whirled and walked rapidly to the edge of camp to be alone.

Men gathered quickly and lifted the injured man; he was too dizzy to stand by himself. Everyone was full of sympathy and the man's wife cried and the children cried.

Then Holly said, "You're lucky he ain't dead."

Everyone stared at him, turning their heads in unison as though this were some movement well rehearsed. Holly waited, chewing his tobacco; finally he spat and said, "You be the only man I ever seen who crossed the Injun-fighter and lived." He let them digest this before going on. "He musta been in one o' them rare good humors, I guess. Well, it's a nice day and the sun's good. I guess he warn't in a killin' mood." He shook his head at the wonder of it all. "I confess I stood there, 'spectin' him to take his knife and carve your guts out thar, feller. It war a surprise to me he just tapped ya lightly. He was just funnin' with ya. Ya know, like you hit your kid a tap to let him know the next'll smart a heap." He laughed softly, a rumbling chuckle.

The injured man shook off the support of his friends and dabbed a handkerchief to his bleeding scalp. "I swear I meant no offense."

"It's jest all this palaver," Holly said. "The Injun-fighter ain't used to it, that's all. He says somethin' an' it's done. This here talk's a bother t'me, but it ain't m'place to rile up about it." He spat again, laughing softly. "I like this to a time when the beaver'n I was up at Taos; I call him beaver thar—it's kinda somethin' 'tween him and me. Wal, as I was sayin' this feller thar hails the Injun-fighter: 'Hey, thar! Where the hell ya goin'!' Well, the beaver he turned about nice as ya please and says, 'Ya speakin' to me, thar?' The feller allowed that he was and they got to cuttin' away right thar. The Injun-fighter plumb whittled him to a twig."

This was too much for the women; even the men were shocked and Holly turned and walked off, heading for the edge of camp where Angevine stood. He sidled up and said, "That feller ain't hurt none."

"I'll apologize to him," Angevine said and would have turned had not Holly taken his arm and held him.

"Oh, now I done fixed it up. Done all that for you." He grinned. "I explained it to 'em and I jest wouldn't make no notice about it, was I you."

"Holly, you're a real friend."

"Man's got to have friends. I took a shine to you right off, beaver."

6

Several times during the balance of the journey, Sergeant Angevine saw smoke and the others saw it too. Holly and Angevine climbed to a high promontory and there built a fire of dry brush and sent up an answering column for no other reason than to confuse the Apaches.

Then Holly dropped the hint around the camp that Angevine had been doing some Apache smoke talk and warning them to stay away. This bit of news made the rounds in a hurry, and as the days passed and no attack came, they came to swear to it. Instead of demonstrating their gratitude, which would have drawn them closer to Angevine, they looked upon him as even more of a stranger with even darker ways and left him more alone.

When they reached Tucson, adobes baking in the sun, Wrigley came to Angevine and said, " 'Preciate what you've done." He didn't offer more, or a handshake; it was finished and he was glad to be shed of it.

The movers established a camp on the south edge of town, and Holly searched out the nearest cantina, for he had an overpowering thirst. Angevine wandered about the town; it was Spanish mostly, with a colony of Americans gaining a strong foothold. Many Indians wandered freely about and he found out that they were Pimas, some shirt-tail kin to the Apaches, but not inclined to be warlike at the moment.

At the store he idled about, looking over the merchandise; much of it had come from Mexico—the leather goods and bright clothing. He found a hat that appealed to him, a *sombrero* with a huge dished brim and bright needlework around the edge. It had an enormous, bullet-shaped crown, and he bought it for three dollars, put it on, and adjusted the chin strap.

His shoes were not a good fit and they were wearing out again, so he bought a pair of Pima moccasins with wrap-arounds up to his knees, such as the Apaches wore, and he found them very light and comfortable.

After he left the store, Angevine searched out Holly and found him in the cantina, a crowd around him and a half a bottle of whisky already under his belt. As soon as Angevine stepped in, Holly stopped talking and everyone turned his head and looked around and then stepped back as Angevine came up to the bar.

"Sergeant McGee is at the stable with the men and horses; we're ready to leave," he said.

"Jes' as soon as I finish this bottle, beaver."

"Take it along or leave it," Angevine told him. "But we've already lost a day and a half with all the stopping every time one of those movers wanted to take a pee. I'm not going to have to explain being late to the major."

"Jes' as you say, thar, beaver." Holly started to pick up the bottle, then thought better of it, shrugged, and sauntered out. Angevine looked around at all the men, not knowing what to make of their watching him so; then he turned and followed Holly out.

One of the Mexicans crossed himself and a husky, round-bellied American blew out a breath and poured himself a drink. "You see those eyes, Harry? Now that Holly don't strike me as no lap cat, but he backed water right now."

"Shore did," another said and had his drink. "I hear he tried to kill one of the movers, but they managed to drag him off. I'd have never bought chips in that. Nosiree."

Another laughed. "Best place for a fella like that is where I ain't."

They agreed to that and all had a drink, and the Americans were so relieved that they invited the Mexicans to join them, forgetting for a moment that they didn't like them.

Everyone returning to Silver City felt better because they didn't have the lumbering, dust-raising wagons along, and the cavalry sergeant formed his men in a column of twos, with Holly and Angevine at the head.

They rode at the alert, carbines in hand, and eternally watched the land about them, for the Apaches did not like to attack alert, well-armed travelers. To hit and kill and run was one thing, but to make a dragged out fight of it and lose men was something the Apaches didn't relish.

Angevine had discovered that at the water hole. They'd fight all right, but they didn't like to see their numbers thinned out. Which made him wonder why they just didn't start out with more. He supposed that for some reason, there weren't many to begin with.

Then, too, with a large party, concealment and surprise would have to be sacrificed.

And that was the Apaches' greatest weapon.

Angevine was bothered by the fact that he knew almost nothing about the Apaches, and no one seemed to know anything. It would have helped if he could know what enraged them so. He found it difficult to believe that they would fight so savagely for only the land because so much of it was arid and useless. Then too, when a people or a nation fought for land, they did so on a larger, more aggressive scale. The Apaches seemed to fight in small raiding parties, and although he found it hard to accept, they seemed to kill only for food and arms.

The escort's return to Silver City was hailed as a great achievement because they hadn't lost a man and a wagon party had gotten through, which meant that the news of that would travel east and more movers would come and perk up the business and bring a greater profit into the tills.

Major Ronald Hoskins, U.S. Cavalry, was very proud of Sergeant McGee and the troopers and rewarded them with a two day pass. Since the paymaster's wagons got through, they had enough to take them on a long drunk and a wild romp on the two-headed beast in the cribs on the north edge of town.

The infantry major had completed the telegraph line to Silver City and was now encamped on the edge of town. He was a little miffed at having missed the to-do made over Sergeant Angevine after his successful fight at the water hole, but now that he had returned bearing further laurels for the troops who moved in a dismounted manner, he personally received his report and congratulated him.

The infantry major felt that the wagons would never have gotten through had not Angevine guided them, and the cavalry major held to the opinion that while Angevine's contribution was considerable, only the presence of McGee's mounted escort held the enemy at length.

This debate seemed pointless to Loch Angevine, who considered himself just plain lucky to have survived any of this. Lieutenant Bascomb was enjoying a period of favor with the commanding officer such as he had never known before, simply because he was Angevine's superior and could modestly say that "I taught the man everything he knows," a blessed phrase which has made famous many men with no talent at all.

Lieutenant Resin Bascomb, after giving a lot of thought to Sergeant Angevine, decided that it would be improper to implore him further to take advantage of his education and seek a commission.

It might be readily granted, over the endorsement of the two majors, and then Angevine would be getting all the credit for his splendid attention to duty and Lieutenant Bascomb would have to hustle more diligently for himself.

So instead, Bascomb offered Angevine the experience and training that only an officer has, offered him friendship and a manner of approach that almost, but not quite, put Angevine as an equal. This was accomplished by taking Angevine into his confidence, an early political device that has served through pages of civilization.

They were in Bascomb's tent and the maps were out and Bascomb was pointing and saying, "By the end of the summer, we want telegraph lines run to Tucson and the military posts that are now under construction there. With a line of communication, we'll soon put the Apaches to their heels."

"What's going to keep the Apaches from cutting the wire, sir?"

Bascomb put down the map and turned to Angevine and stared, as a father will when his beautiful lecture has been spoiled irrevocably by a stupid observation. "Sergeant, the cavalry at each of the posts will be charged with patrolling the line. That seems obvious to me." He turned again to the map, then thought of something else. "Besides, we are dealing with primitive savages who do not have the intelligence to grasp the meaning of the wire. They will leave it alone because they are superstitious."

"Yes, sir, but they'll learn, just like sailors learned that the world wasn't flat."

"Sergeant, I do not care to debate this! Understand?"

"Yes, sir."

"Our job is to survey on to Tucson, and since you have already been through the pass, your knowledge of the terrain ahead will be most valuable. I would like to have you prepare a written report. Don't sign it. It will look better if it goes to the major's desk over my signature. Please be thorough in your description of the terrain and conditions of the various springs and camp sites. Also include your estimate of the degree of hostile activity in that area."

"Yes, sir."

"One more thing . . . Mr. Holly. The major and I have discussed the matter and we are both concerned about his drinking habits. Civilian scouts are always a problem and Mr. Holly was all that was available. He seems capable, but he is just not military in his manner and morals. I would like to know how you get along with him."

"Fine, sir. Holly and I are good friends. He's taught me a great deal, sir."

"Very well, we'll let the matter pass for the time being."

"Will that be all, sir?"

"Yes. Go into town and get Holly and see that he stays sober. The major wants the survey crew to leave as soon as possible. I think early tomorrow morning should please him. And, sergeant—don't you think your manner of dress a bit whimsical?"

"Sir?"

"Never mind," Bascomb said, waving his hand. "As the major pointed out, it does remind the civilians that we are here and doing a grand job. Carry on, sergeant."

Angevine saluted and got out of the tent, feeling

relieved and wondering why because the lieutenant was an all right fellow. He went into town and looked around a few of the saloons, trying to find Holly. Silver City's streets were just not wide enough to handle the wagons and mounted traffic, and the walks were clogged with miners and toughs and citizens trying to lead a normal life where normalcy was out of the question.

He supposed that his dress did set him apart from the others, but the hat was marvelous for shade and the high crown kept his head cool in the hottest sun and the Indian leggings were better than any shoes he had ever worn.

Holly was holding council in the largest saloon and he had a good audience to keep pouring the drinks. Angevine shouldered his way through and Holly stopped talking and swayed like a wind-stirred tree. He looked at Angevine and said, "Beaver, what ya want?"

"We're going back to camp."

"Hell, I jest got here!" He shook his head. "I ain't goin'. Got a lot of drinkin' to do."

Everyone stood quietly as though they were holding their breath, and Angevine laid his Henry repeater on the bar. "You've got to be sober tomorrow, Holly, so you're going back now. We got to go back to Tucson."

"Through that 'er pass?" Holly said.

"Through the pass," Angevine repeated.

Holly scratched his beard and stared thoughtfully at the floor. "Beaver, I don't hanker to do that. Do I got to?"

95

"Lieutenant's orders. He's coming too." He reached out and grabbed Holly's sleeve and the scout tried to jerk away, but Angevine expected it and pushed him back against the bar. "Holly, I'll carry you out if I have to." With his free hand he scooped up his rifle and Holly stepped uncertainly away from the bar and headed for the door, Angevine right behind him, still holding onto his arm.

Going out, they bumped smack-dab into two miners coming in and the miners reared back, mightily offended by this rudeness. One brushed Holly to one side, then stopped when Angevine raised the muzzle of the rifle slightly; it was a reflex action, for he meant to use it to ward off any blow that came his way.

"Hold 'er there!" the miner said, palms out. "No offense meant now." He stepped aside and his friend got Holly straightened around and then the miners hurried on inside and Angevine steered Holly unsteadily on down the street and out of town to the camp.

Holly sang on the way there and laughed and staggered around, then when Angevine dumped him on his robes, the scout fell immediately to sleep, snoring loudly.

It embarrassed Angevine to see his friend like this, without pride, and he wondered what made Holly do it. Demon rum, he supposed, as the temperance people always preached. It got to a man, ate away his will, destroyed his character; yet standing there, looking at Holly, dirty and unshaven, it was hard to imagine that he had ever been any other way.

There was not much about Holly, Angevine had to admit, that could be called a saving grace. Yet he was a man of courage, fearless, prudent, knowing of the wild ways, and in this country those were the things that really mattered. A man's knowledge of literature and art did him no good here.

He spent the rest of that day making ready to leave in the morning, but toward evening the stage from the east arrived, and although Angevine didn't go into town to see it arrive and had no interest in it, the arrival changed everything for him.

There were two passengers, a Mrs. Bowen, and her daughter, Eleanor, the family of a lieutenant colonel stationed at Camp Yuma. The good lady, in defiance of War Department policy, intended to go on and join her Lucius there and would tolerate no delay.

Lieutenant Bascomb, when informed of this, went into a funk and hastily reported to the infantry major for orders. And the infantry major, after swearing profusely, went to the cavalry major and with flattery and lies, persuaded the cavalry major to provide escort and thus relieved himself of the nasty responsibility.

Mrs. Bowen and daughter were put up at the hotel. She was a large-boned woman who in ten minutes had blistered the hotel boy for clumsily handling her luggage, harangued the hotel owner for having an untidy place, and called mightily for the senior officer, for she intended to give him a piece of her mind.

The daughter was a demure girl with flaxen hair and

a very quiet manner; she seemed a bit embarrassed by all the commotion her mother stirred up, but by training held to her silence. It was her smile, a quick, compassionate lifting of the lips given behind her mother's back that saved the hotel boy's pride and the owner's temper.

Since Lieutenant Colonel Bowen was cavalry, the cavalry major was called and was indeed dressed down; he took it very well, a little tight-lipped and pinched about the eyes, but well.

Her spleen vented, Mrs. Bowen recounted all the irritating delays in stage travel and wanted to know when she could leave for Camp Yuma, having no idea of the distance or traveling conditions.

The major quickly explained the dangers from Apache attack and Mrs. Bowen gave him her opinion by saying, "Agh!" and pointedly looking out the window at the untidy town. So the major bit his lip a moment, then began to make some suggestions. The telegraph had to go through on schedule or there would be the devil to pay, so he couldn't disrupt the progress to provide an escort of two companies.

Mrs. Bowen assured him that this was all right with her, for she had no intention of having her daughter's privacy disturbed by the coarseness of enlisted men. It seemed to her that if a stage could get through to Silver City, a similar vehicle could get through to Camp Yuma. Perhaps a small escort would be tolerable but not a company.

Her views were as firm as only a field grade

officer's wife's can be. She would not stay in Silver City. She would go on, without fear, certain that no Indian would be fool enough to harm the wife of an officer in the United States Army.

The major's mind was in a whirl; arguing with her was like kicking a Chinese gong: the result was not melodious but deafening. In the end he got her to agree that a stage with leather curtains, six troopers, and two men as scouts would be the minimum escort that conscience would permit. After all, he would have to answer to her husband for her safety.

This decision was accepted, not particularly gracefully, and Mrs. Bowen declared that she would be ready to leave as soon as she and her daughter had bathed and changed clothes.

He left the hotel, returned to his headquarters a bit shaken, and immediately had Lieutenant Bascomb summoned. It wouldn't do, he explained, to have the escort in the charge of an enlisted man, for Mrs. Bowen would not know how to talk to him. And since he could spare none of the cavalry officers, it would fall on Lieutenant Bascomb to take charge. Mrs. Bowen could relate to him all her complaints, which he would duly note and include in a report later.

Bascomb left the major's tent a bit shaken and had Sergeant Angevine report and he explained just how it was going to be. He wanted Angevine to pick six soldiers known to be excellent shots and have them ride with the driver and atop the coach. Holly also would have to be completely sober with no trace of whisky on his breath.

Angevine left Bascomb's tent a bit shaken, the tremor having passed on down the line.

They were to leave that evening at dusk, for Angevine felt that the cool of night would make for the best traveling, and a full moon would be out and he did not think that the Indians would attack at night.

He had much to do, selecting soldiers and beating down their protests since they were all picked "volunteers". Again he had them armed with shotguns and revolvers and saw that they had plenty of ammunition. Rations were drawn, every detail checked and rechecked, and then they assembled and accompanied the coach into town and drew up in front of the hotel where Mrs. Bowen descended like royalty about to attend the ball. And the daughter trailed her, smiling a little smile as if to say that mother was really a brick, just overbearing as hell.

She looked long at Loch Angevine and Holly and she smiled at Angevine, who nodded pleasantly and handed her into the coach and closed the door. Lieutenant Bascomb rode up, splendidly mounted, and he motioned for both Angevine and Holly to mount.

Mrs. Bowen, noticing the soldiers atop the coach, stuck her head out and said, "What are those soldiers doing up there? Get them off!"

Bascomb was polite. "The coach, madam, and its precious cargo is what we wish to protect. Besides, as we get into the pass, mounted men would do us no real service." He waved the driver on and the coach lurched and Mrs. Bowen cracked her head against the window frame and people cheered and they bolted out of town, scattering traffic.

Holly and Angevine took the point and they moved right along, the coach pitching and tossing along behind. For an hour they stuck to this pace but finally brought everything to a walk to cool the horses.

The first housekeeping stop was called by Mrs. Bowen. She berated Angevine and Bascomb in thunderous indignation because proper screening had not been provided; they were in brushy, open country and Lieutenant Bascomb, trained to emergencies, called the men to attention, made them execute an about-face, and kept them there while the women tended to private matters.

Still Mrs. Bowen was fretful; she felt that since the soldiers knew what they were doing, it was just as bad as watching and she promised to inform her husband of this.

Loch Angevine, having now heard her complain, both as to volume and frequency, decided that she must be joining her husband to torture him, or at least convince him that his military burden was nothing, really.

Eleanor, the daughter, smiled at him every time he looked at her and once her mother caught her and gave her the very devil. Thereafter Angevine watched himself carefully so as not to cause the girl any trouble again.

Full darkness was a blessing, for an hour later the heat began to fade. By midnight there was a pronounced chill to the air and Mrs. Bowen wanted to stop and build a fire, a bit of foolishness no one thought to take seriously. This was a mistake for considerable fuss was made until Lieutenant Bascomb informed her about the dangers of fires in Apache country.

In the still hours before dawn they arrived at a small water hole, no more than a seep, and made camp for a few hours' rest. A tent was pitched for Mrs. Bowen and her daughter, a small soldiers' tent that she found completely inadequate, but since that was all that was available, they entered, flapped it tightly and the good lady was heard no more that night.

The soldiers slept in pairs while the others stood guard, and when dawn approached, all were quietly wakened and alerted. This had been Angevine's suggestion and he had Bascomb put the soldiers atop the coach and inside it so that the camp looked deserted. He and Holly bellied down under the coach so that it would look as though they were still sleeping.

A gray light began to seep into the sky when Angevine touched Holly gently on the arm and drew his attention to a clump of mesquite sixty yards away. Two Apaches left that cover and came on in a crouch.

Holly nodded, then pointed in a quartering direction; two more were closing in on the spring. He tapped himself and pointed to the right, indicating that he would handle those, and Angevine shouldered his Henry rifle.

The shot was startling in the stillness, but he hit one Apache squarely and sent him asprawl. Holly opened fire and it seemed that each clump of brush erupted into Indians. From the coach there was a smashing pound of shotguns and this took the Apaches completely by surprise; they hadn't realized that the main force was inside and atop the coach.

Mrs. Bowen let out a long, piercing scream and Holly said, "God damn anyway!"

Then Angevine saw that Mrs. Bowen was trying to get out of the tent in her panic and he knew she couldn't do that and live more than ten or fifteen seconds.

Bolting from his cover, he dashed over, launched himself and landed belly and knees on the tent, crushing the women flat and holding them there by his weight. They fought and wiggled and he pushed with his hands and bumped with his knees and the shotguns pounded away and the Apaches fell back, leaving the dead and bearing off the wounded.

Then the shooting stopped completely and the daylight kept getting stronger and Bascomb jumped down and Loch Angevine got up and stepped back.

Holly was out there, looking at the Apaches; he put a bullet into one who was playing dead. The soldiers reloaded their shotguns and at Bascomb's order, remained alert in case there was another attack. Then he came over while Angevine was trying to find the tent flap amid the tangle of pulled rope and canvas.

Mrs. Bowen finally emerged, sticking her head out;

she was in a fury, a positive pinnacle of rage, and since Resin Bascomb was an officer, she directed it all at him. She wanted the name of the beast who had crushed them, manhandled them. She wanted the names of the soldiers for she felt that all of them had been negligent in their duty, allowing the Apaches to get this close.

She wanted a lot of things and finally Bascomb lost his temper. "Madam," he said frostily, "kindly shut your mouth!"

Her gasp sounded like wind moaning in a deep cave and she was too horrified to speak immediately, which gave Bascomb a chance. "We have saved your life, madam, and if you lack the grace to appreciate it, then have the courtesy to remain silent while we do our work."

Then he pivoted on his heel, barked orders rapidly, and ten minutes later they were loaded and leaving the spring and the five dead Apaches.

Angevine's confidence in Bascomb as an officer and a gentleman was thus richly increased.

7

The encounter with the Apaches had been Lieutenant Bascomb's first, not only with the Apaches but with any hostile Indians, and it had badly shaken him, at a time when he could not afford to be shaken.

Riding along now he reflected on his words to Mrs.

Bowen, and he regretted them. They were true enough and he had certainly been sincere, but he had lost his grasp of the situation completely and given way to his personal feelings, a mistake an officer could not afford to make.

The fight had been brief and vicious, a spasm of terror in his mind, and reflecting on it now, he could only thank Providence for making him listen to Angevine in the first place and station himself and his men inside the coach. He thought of Angevine: the damned little bulldog, dashing out there to the women without a fear in the world. If he hadn't pounced on that tent and kept them in it, the Apaches would likely have killed either or both of them and then the fat would have been in the fire.

I should have done that, Bascomb thought.

Sergeant Angevine rode behind the coach, braving the dust although he stayed just far enough back to keep out of the worst of it. The sun was climbing and the day promised to be full of smothering heat with no cooling breeze.

Holly was out front, the point, and that suited Angevine because he didn't feel like talking to Holly or having the lieutenant look at him either. He'd really pulled a fool play, bolting the way he had and jumping on the women in the tent. And he hadn't meant to be rough with them, but the Apaches had scared the peewaddin' out of him and he'd just plain lost his head. And it bothered him to know that he'd thought only of the young one with her smile and he hadn't cared at all what happened to the old battle-axe.

He'd sure been a fool all right, dashing out there like that. The lieutenant had kept his head, and Holly hadn't panicked; they had realized that by staying down and shooting, they could do more to help the women than by running out there. He'd known that too. Knew it when they took their positions around the coach and left the women sleeping peacefully in the tent.

But know it or not, he'd broken and done the fool thing and the fact that he was still alive was a matter of blind luck and nothing more. And he didn't want to ride with Holly and have the scout remind him of it, or to look back at the lieutenant and find him watching him. All he could hope for was that the women had not been able to tell who had crushed the tent and handled them so roughly.

Inside the coach, the leather curtains drawn, Mrs. Bowen kept up a ceaseless rattle of complaint. She sat in one corner, bracing herself against the constant buck and lurch, fanning herself and giving vocal vent to her suffering. She was dedicated to it, in love with it, and Eleanor, sitting across from her, opened the petcock of her mind and let this barrage of words drain through without actually hearing any of it.

She still felt a bit shaken over the events at dawn; the sudden shooting had given her a terrible start, but it had frightened her mother immeasurably worse. The older woman had panicked completely and tried to get out of the tent and Eleanor had grabbed her, but her strength had been no match at all and her mother would have broken free had not Sergeant Angevine saved them.

She was sure he had been the one because when the shooting stopped, he had immediately pulled her free of the tent folds and helped her to her feet. Her mother had not noticed this; one of the blessings of anger was blindness.

Perhaps, before this journey was over, she would have a chance to speak to him alone. But that was hardly likely, for her mother had all the instincts of a county jailer.

When they reached Camp Yuma, Eleanor promised herself that she would speak to her father in Lieutenant Bascomb's behalf, for she knew that her mother would never forgive him for the way he had spoken.

Still her mother had shut up as far as the escort was concerned, for a time anyway. Shock will do that sometimes.

By midday, the heat was so intense that Mrs. Bowen was forced to open the leather curtains, dust or not. She shouted at Bascomb and ordered him to stop at the first handy stream so they could bathe and refresh themselves, and Lt. Bascomb announced, with a certain wicked pleasure, that the nearest water was some thirty miles further.

The water, when they reached it shortly before nightfall, was a small seep that held barely enough to refill their canteens and supply cooking water. What little remained, Bascomb permitted the women to use to wash, and they could only wet cloths and wash their faces.

Again, Bascomb insisted upon the strictest guard precautions and would not permit the women to stray from camp regardless of Mrs. Bowen's demands for privacy. Realizing that argument would accomplish nothing, Bascomb said, "Madam, the Apaches have watched us every step of the way, and right now they lurk out there, waiting for someone to stray away from the well-guarded camp. And I understand that they prize women most highly for slaves."

Mrs. Bowen lost all desire to leave the camp and Bascomb privately thought that this was indeed a pity, for if the Apaches captured her and some luckless brave took her for a wife, she would raise so much hell that it might cure them of ever molesting a white woman again.

Mrs. Bowen was very selfishly denying peace and comfort to the settlers of Arizona Territory.

When it came time to pitch the tent, Mrs. Bowen set up a howl of protest; no one was going to get her into that thing again. Bascomb solved it by simply saying, ". . . that the rattlesnakes would never crawl into the tent. However, if madam insisted . . ."

Mrs. Bowen *did* insist . . . on sleeping in the tent.

After the evening meal, the fire was allowed to die, for Bascomb wanted it out when darkness came. He did not like the camp site; they had just crowded between two walls of rock and passed through the most forbidding terrain, and they were camped on the eastern downslope of a summit on reasonably open ground.

Finally he went over to where Angevine sat and said, "Sergeant, when are we going to reach Apache Pass?"

"You just went through it, sir."

This made Bascomb feel like a fool and he became angry. "Where in hell is the spring then?"

"About a half a mile down the slope, in a grove of trees."

"Sergeant, I do not appreciate this cavalier action without consulting me. Please explain yourself."

"Yes, sir. Well, I got to thinking today, riding back there. When the Apaches hit us just before dawn, I don't think they knew we had women along. But Mrs. Bowen screamed, and they found out. I know you were just trying to scare Mrs. Bowen, sir, but you hit it right when you said that the Apaches had been following us. My guess is that they let us get through the pass and intended to hit us when we camped at the spring. Which is why I picked this seep, sir. They're down there now, waiting."

"Are you certain of this, sergeant?"

"I've never been certain of anything, sir," Angevine said. "But I hung back all day and watched the high ground. Apaches make mistakes the same as we do, sir, and once or twice I saw a little dust."

"This afternoon, when we were working up through the pass, that would have been the best place to attack," Bascomb said. "Why didn't they?"

"I figure it's too much of a risk for them because they didn't want to kill the women, sir."

Bascomb nodded. "All right, that sounds right. But you think they are waiting at the spring?"

"Yes, sir. They figured we'd make for the water and splash around a bit. I remember how the movers were, sir, like a bunch of kids, ready to relax and have fun. And that's the way the Apaches wanted us, sir, spending more time enjoying ourselves than standing guard."

"Sergeant, that's good thinking. All right, I expect we'd better move the men into the coach and get ready for another welcome." He started to get up, but Angevine put out his hand and touched him, holding him there.

"Sir, I've been in three brushes with Apaches, and all three times they've attacked the same way, just before dawn, working in close and then rushing us."

"So? That's the way they fight, that's all. Obvious to me."

"Yes, sir. But it makes me wonder if they don't figure we always fight the same way too. I mean, we camp and put out a guard. They expect it, sir."

"I don't see what you're getting at, sergeant."

"Well, sir, we put the women in your tent and hid in the coach. It's my guess, sir, that they'll figure we'll do the same thing again because it worked once. I'd like to suggest, sir, that we roll up our blankets and put them atop the coach, and under it, like we were waiting there. We could cut some sticks that would

110

look like rifle barrels. Then I'd put the men in the rocks above the camp; we can cover it with cross fire that way. If we move the coach over toward the downslope, the Apaches would have to come in that way, up the rise, crawling through the brush. When they hit the coach—"

"By God, that's good, sergeant," Bascomb said, forgetting for a moment that he was a superior officer, by training and instincts. "But won't they go for the women right away?"

"I don't think so, sir. They'd want to do us in first. The women would give them no fight after we were gone, sir."

"All right, sergeant, we'll follow your plan. You and Holly take care of placing the men where you want them, but I'm going to remain in the coach. An ace in the hole."

Loch Angevine thought this was very foolish, but also very brave; it was the kind of a thing an officer would do, but he would never have done it, which was why he knew that he was not a leader.

A man in the coach, to put up a token fight, would convince the Apaches that all the men were there and give their defense a tremendous advantage. Yet to remain alone in the coach was very dangerous and Bascomb was risking his life.

Holly, since the dawn fight, had taken on a spell of solitude, as though he were sick of the world and would just as soon be shed of it. Angevine had taken his mess tin over and tried to join Holly in the evening meal, but the scout got up and walked to another place. This had hurt Angevine, but he said nothing, figuring that Holly was disgusted with Angevine's foolishness in jumping on the tent. Loch wondered what he could do, and decided that doing nothing certainly could not help.

Holly had made a place for himself by the coach and Angevine went over to him; it was too dark to see him clearly, so he said, "We're moving into the rocks, Holly."

"You done cozyin' up to the officers?" He laughed softly. "Got yer sign now, beaver. Makin' a name fer yerself with the wimmen so's the officers'll pat you on the head."

Angevine was thoroughly bewildered and began to be annoyed.

"That's not so, Holly. What's the matter with you? I thought we were friends."

"The sky's my friend, beaver. The wind's company enough fer me. I took to you, beaver. You know I did. Even in the times of the fur trade and the rondeevoos I never took to a feller like I done you."

Perhaps it was his weariness or the situation— Angevine never knew—but his patience snapped. "Holly, don't lie to me anymore."

Holly slowly stood up. "Lie?"

"Yes, lie," Angevine said. "When we first met, I told a lie and you caught me in it. But you've spun some pretty tall stories, Holly, and I never said anything about them. Most of them I believed, but I was only believing what I wanted to believe."

"No man calls me a liar, boy."

"Holly, we're friends. Don't put on for me about the fur trade and all the country you've scouted. You told me you'd been through Apache Pass, but it wasn't so." He sighed. "You're a good man, Holly. Can't we let it go at that?"

"Thar be 'Paches about," Holly said softly, "and I need you a-shootin.' But come Tucson, beaver, I'll be settlin' this with you. It won't do to have you goin' about sayin' ol' Holly's a liar, boy. Won't do at all. Hell, you kilt a couple o' Injuns and now you're big beaver. People say 'hidy' to you and git off the walk when they see you comin'. Wal, I made you, boy, and I can unmake you just as easy." He reached out and bumped Angevine on the chest. "Come Tucson I'll show everbody you ain't nothin' 'tall."

"What's got into you, Holly? Hell, man, you think I'm not scared? I've been scared of something or other all my life. I never tried to pretend I wasn't. Hell, it's all right to spin those windies of yours in a saloon and cadge a drink or two, but we're friends and there's no need you telling me all the time about Hugh Glass and all that bullshit because I like you just the way you are."

"I'll say no more," Holly snapped. "I want no truck with you."

He picked up his rifle and passed on, bumping Angevine solidly with his shoulder.

Angevine stood there, confused and angry and he

113

tried to understand Holly, but it always came around to one thing: Holly just couldn't bear having been found out. It had to be that, but it didn't seem like enough to fight over.

But Tucson was a good distance away and in that time Holly might change his mind. At least that was Angevine's hope.

Very quietly, he went around to the soldiers and got them into positions in the rocks and warned them to make absolutely no sound at all and not to fire until he did or Lieutenant Bascomb did from the coach.

The night was dark; the moon wouldn't be up until late, which suited Angevine. He had no doubt that the soldiers would sleep because they were pretty frazzled, and it really didn't matter as long as someone stayed awake.

That would be his job, and Bascomb's, so he settled down to another miserable night. He didn't know where Holly was and this bothered him, for he and the scout had always stuck close together. Now he was alone and he told himself that it didn't matter because he didn't need Holly, yet he wondered if Holly felt the same way.

There was no sound at all from the tent; the women slept soundly.

In the dark silence, Angevine thought of home. It seemed like a long time since he had seen it, and he wondered what it would be like to go back now. Thinking back on his first months of service, everything seemed hazy, as though his vision had partially failed him. He could not remember details, just impressions. It rather surprised him to find that he knew the names of only two men from that time— Sergeant Gore and Lieutenant Bascomb.

He wondered why that was and finally decided that his attention and thoughts had been so concentrated on what he was doing and how he was doing it that he hadn't had time to see anyone else or anything he did not have to see. Gore and Bascomb, his immediate superiors, were the ones he had had to please, so he knew them well. It was a feeling he was familiar with from the years of having tried to please his father. The difference was that with the lieutenant he seemed to have succeeded. This brought him back to Holly and the man's absurd jealousy, and with this thought it occurred to Angevine that he must in fact have changed considerably for he was able to recognize the foolishness in a man and not despise him. He realized also that he did not need Holly as much as he had first thought.

I've got two feet of my own to stand on, Loch Angevine thought, and decided then and there that if Holly wanted to fight in Tucson, he'd not have to look far for it.

And if he wanted to forget it and go on being friends, he could do that too.

It was one and the same to Sergeant Loch Angevine.

Mrs. Bowen, driven from her tent by an irresistible urge of nature, woke the entire camp by bellowing for Lieutenant Bascomb. She stood in plain sight, a target for any Apache lurking about, shouting, "Mr. Bascomb, do—you—hear—me?"

Indeed Bascomb heard her; her voice probably carried halfway down the pass and across the spring on the other side.

There was nothing Bascomb could do but leave the coach; he came over and said, "Madam, I implore you to lower your voice. What is it?"

"What do you think one wakes up in the middle of the night for? To look at the moon? What are you going to do about it? I must have some privacy."

Angevine left his place among the rocks and swept up some brush and started a roaring fire. He called to the soldiers to help him and soon they had a huge fire going; it pushed back the darkness for a considerable distance.

"What are you doing?" Mrs. Bowen demanded.

"Madam, they are trying to light the area so that the Apaches will hesitate to attack. They have been watching us all night, and thanks to your inopportune—appearance, they now know exactly where we were waiting." He motioned to several soldiers. "Please get your blankets and surround Mrs. Bowen so she can empty her damned bladder."

"Well!" she said, aghast. "Your impertinence will not go unreported, Mr. Bascomb!"

He turned away from her and urged the other soldiers to heap more brush on the fire until it mounted furiously and he stood there with his pistol in hand, along with Angevine who had his rifle cocked and ready.

The soldiers held up the blankets and surrounded Mrs. Bowen and Eleanor thrust her head out of the tent but drew back when Angevine said, "Please remain inside, miss."

She smiled and disappeared and Bascomb said, "Sergeant," and drew Angevine's attention across the clearing. An Apache showed himself but he held his rifle high. "Hold your fire," Bascomb said, and the soldiers cradled their shotguns while three more Apaches showed themselves.

The leader was a giant of a man, well over six feet two and well on in years. He had a broad, cruel face and no fear in him at all, for he walked toward the fire, his weapon raised.

Bascomb said, "Corporal Towers, when Mrs. Bowen has completed her duty, please remain with the blanket around her." He turned to the Apache and took some cigars from his shirt pocket and offered them, but the Indian acted as though he did not see them nor the outstretched hand. Bascomb's face took on color and he returned the cigars to his pocket. "Holly, come here and see if you can talk to this beggar. Holly?"

"I don't see him around, sir," Angevine said.

"How in the devil do you talk to a man whose language you don't speak?" Bascomb asked.

"I speak," the Apache said and surprised the devil out of all of them. "I am Coloradas."

"And I am Lieutenant Resin Bascomb, United States Army. Where did you learn to speak English? I didn't know there was a school aro—"

117

"Long ago, white man come into mountains of my people. Dig in ground for metal. I learn speak. Many my people learn speak." He waved his arm. "This my land. One time we not harm white man. He kill, beat my people. All white man bad. You no come through land."

"We only want to pass through," Bascomb said. "We won't harm you if you don't harm us."

"You speak for all white man?" He tapped himself on the chest. "I speak for all my people. Make word. Keep word. White man make word, other white man not know word. Break word. You go through. Tell all your people not come this way."

With that he turned and walked away, and in a moment they were gone as they had come, without a sound and without warning. Lieutenant Bascomb blew out a long breath and holstered his pistol.

The corporal in charge of the blanket detail said, "Is it all right to secure now, sir?"

"Oh, damn it, yes," Bascomb said, irritated because he had forgotten about it.

During this longest period of wakeful silence in her life, Mrs. Bowen had thought up a series of new complaints. She came up, eyes brittle. "Mr. Bascomb, why didn't you kill those savages?"

"They came into the camp with their weapons raised, madam."

"You honor their word, sir?"

"I'm afraid, madam, that Coloradas is quite correct in saying that while he speaks for all the Apaches, I

118

hardly am able to speak for myself. And since you have favored us with your delightful company, madam, I have hardly been able to speak without interrupting you. Now please retire to your tent."

"I am quite rested, thank you."

"I'm sure you are, madam, but I'm quite weary of your tongue, your questions, and your incessant whining. And I will be glad to so state that to your husband when I meet him."

She was too angry to speak, so she crawled back into the tent, not a dignified maneuver at best. Bascomb saw Holly standing at the farthest reach of light and he said, "Come over here, Holly. Where the devil were you when I called you?"

"In them thar rocks," Holly said dryly. "When there's 'Paches about, I'm keepin' m'eyes open. I had a bead on Coloradas' breastbone all the time he was talkin,' and he knowed it too."

"Well," Bascomb said, "I don't suppose I can find genuine fault with your caution, Holly."

"Didn't think you would thar." He bit off a chew of tobacco. "Was I you, I'd move on down to the spring. Be daylight soon and the wimmen can bathe and do all them things wimmen do."

"The idea is sound," Bascomb said, and went about giving the orders.

Angevine said, "Holly, I've been hoping that mood you were in—"

"Warn't no mood at all, beaver. You'n me's plumb wore it out, that's all. Settlin' time's come. If'n I don't,

119

you'll soon start tellin' lies about ol' Holly. Sayin' he's full of hot air and such. Folks step light about me, beaver. When they start forgettin,' I go an' put me down a man to remind 'em." He started to turn away but Angevine suddenly reached out and jerked him around. Holly raised his rifle by instinct and Angevine half expected it and knocked it clean out of his hands. It whipped around, spun twice, and landed on the ground ten feet away.

Then Holly's eyes got round and cautious and he stood there, waiting to see what was going to happen next. Angevine said, "Listen to me, Holly! I'd rather run than fight and give in before arguing, but damn it man, don't make the mistake of thinking that I'm yellow. I never meant you any harm, by act or talk. Don't press a fight with me. There's no need for it."

"Ain't there? You put your hands on me, beaver. No backin' off now." He nodded and Angevine was suddenly aware that all the soldiers had stopped and were watching him. Holly nodded. "Got to now, don't I? Can't have 'em sayin' they seen me back water from any man. That's the way the stick floats."

Then he walked over and picked up his fallen rifle and went to get his sleeping robes.

8

Tucson was a welcome relief, for here Lieutenant Bascomb intended to lay over two days and refresh the supplies, rest the horses, give the soldiers a chance to break the monotony of the march, and allow Mrs. Bowen to vent her poison on the luckless hotel keeper.

Bascomb knew that he could not consider the miles yet ahead of them unless his mind was conditioned and rosied by several shots of whisky, so he hied forth to the nearest saloon and began drinking. This was not a habit of Bascomb's. In fact, he was a very sober man, rather against hard liquids of any kind, and just one step from joining the Temperance League. Such virtue could not escape unnoticed or go unrewarded, and as the talkative bartender poured, he informed Lieutenant Bascomb that Colonel Bowen and a large detail was already in town, having made the trip from Yuma earlier in the week.

Had Bascomb been jumped ten places on the promotion list he could not have been happier. He laid money on the bar and told the bartender to drink it himself, then bolted out of the place, intent on finding Bowen and telling him the happy news.

The Lieutenant Colonel was at the newly constructed telegraph office; the line had already been surveyed and put up between Tucson and Camp Yuma and awaited the final link-up to Fort Union and points east. He was a robust man, fifty-some, with a round, pleasant face and a well-fed look about him.

Seeing a strange lieutenant was a bit of a surprise; Bowen recovered quickly and answered Bascomb's salute and shook his hand and was very jolly about it all until Bascomb informed Bowen as to why he had a detail in Tucson.

"Claudia here?" Bowen bellowed and went so far as to seize the Lieutenant's arm, shaking it furiously. "Man, it can't be. My God, what are you saying?"

"She is at the hotel now, sir. Your daughter is with her."

"My daughter?" He sounded as though he had to be reminded that he had a daughter. "She's supposed to be happily married!"

"I don't know anything about that, sir," Bascomb said. "Would you care to receive my report now?"

"I'd like a drink of whisky and a transfer," Bowen said. He wiped a trembling hand across his forehead. "At the hotel, you say? Well, I might as well welcome her to Arizona." He offered his hand again to Bascomb. "I know you've had an experience, my boy. She'd rout the devil out of his own bed if she were tired and wanted to stretch out."

"Colonel, I would like to say that I exceeded my authority and spoke very harshly to Mrs. Bowen. I am prepared to answer any charges you—"

"Nonsense," Bowen said, and went out, squaring himself a little as he passed through the doorway. Then he marched resolutely up the street toward the hotel.

Sergeant Loch Angevine remained with his men and Holly disappeared as soon as they reached town. After the evening meal, Angevine left the soldiers' camp and walked into the town; he had a hanker for a few things at the store and made his purchases before doing his strolling up and down the street. In the back of his mind lurked the awareness that Holly was about somewhere, getting dangerous, but it was not a genuine worry, just something he would have to take care of when the time came. He wasn't sure what he would do, but he hoped that Holly would change his mind and not get violent.

A soldier from Colonel Bowen's command hailed Angevine, and he stopped while the soldier came up. "Sergeant, the Lieutenant Colonel wants to see you at the hotel. He's in the dining room."

"Now?"

"Right now," the soldier said. "I've been looking for you for fifteen minutes."

Angevine nodded, turned, and walked toward the hotel. The dining room was just off the lobby, a rather small room with low ceiling beams and calcimined adobe walls. Mrs. Bowen's expression was prim, her lips pressed tightly together as though someone had been trying to feed her something she didn't like and hadn't yet given up all resistance. Eleanor looked at Angevine as he approached and smiled sweetly. Colonel Bowen looked around and Angevine came to attention and saluted.

"At ease, sergeant. My daughter informs me that your services on the trip were invaluable and if it hadn't been for you, certain disaster would have befallen the party."

"I appreciate the compliment, sir, but my contribution was only very slight. My fear of the Apaches prompted me to take unusual precautions."

"It's well that you did, sergeant. Lieutenant Bascomb informs me that he has not yet identified the man who pounced on Mrs. Bowen while she was in her tent."

"The lieutenant was quite busy fighting Indians, sir," Angevine said. "However, I am the one you seek, sir. Had Mrs. Bowen and her daughter emerged, sir, I'm sure they would have been killed."

"My own conclusion exactly," Bowen said.

"And one I do not share," Mrs. Bowen snapped. "Lucius, are you going to put the sergeant on report or not?"

"My dear, I am not. As a matter of fact, I'm going to write the sergeant up in a dispatch. That will be all, sergeant."

"Thank you, sir." He saluted, did an about-face, and went out to stand on the porch. The night was turning very cool and lamplight spilled from windows and doorways. Down the street, in some cantina, he heard Holly's wild whoop, and from the tenor of it he knew that Holly was getting dangerously drunk. Right now he was shooting off his mouth but a little later, when he'd had just the right amount to drink, he'd shoot his gun if provoked.

Considering the way Holly felt, Loch Angevine knew that he had no further obligation to the man, but he couldn't just abandon Holly. Holly was in a mean frame of mind and he was liable to knife someone, and if it wasn't a fair fight, he could get hung for it. Angevine wasn't about to stand by and let that happen.

So he walked down the street to the cantina and pushed the swinging doors open, stopping just inside. Holly was at the bar and he looked around and saw Angevine standing there, and without warning he bounded away, hit the floor in a roll, and fired his rifle as he came up. Hurry and liquor spoiled his aim slightly, and the bullet zipped past Angevine's ear, barely touching the tip and drawing a little blood.

Angevine flung himself back from the doorway and went against the wall, then he darted down the street and cut over as Holly came charging out. He flung two fast shots at Angevine, but in the darkness he could not see too well and Angevine was a moving target; the whisky did the rest and Angevine ducked safely into a doorway as Holly's last shot dimpled the adobe.

Angevine yelled, "Holly, you damned fool, cut it out now!"

Lieutenant Bascomb ran out of the store and saw what was happening. Holly swung his rifle and took a shot at him and drove Bascomb back inside. The people who had been out scattered and the street was empty save for Angevine in the doorway and Holly crouched by the cantina wall.

Holly, protected by a stout post, shouted, "I can wait as long as you can, beaver!"

"For God's sake, Holly! I thought you wanted a fair fight. What the hell are you shooting at me for?" Angevine yelled.

" 'Cuz I said I would!"

Farther down, Bascomb reappeared, this time with a squad of soldiers. He yelled, "Holly, put down your arms and surrender!"

Angevine felt a great sense of relief. This was the right way to deal with that crazy, drunken lunatic.

But Holly immediately swung around and fired and one of the soldiers fell, clutching his thigh. Bascomb needed no further prodding. "Fire!" he said, and ran forward, shooting his pistol.

The soldiers fanned out and Holly was driven from his place. He took three steps, whirled and shot one more time. Then a ragged volley tore him down and put him in the gutter.

Angevine left his place by the door and dashed across the street; Bascomb was already there, kicking Holly's rifle out of reach in case there was any life left in him. People reappeared and one man came out of a store with a lantern and held it high so they could all see how badly Holly had been shot through. Angevine looked carefully at the broken body, vacant eyes, and the dark blood just beginning to clot. He felt only a wild sense of disbelief.

Turning, he looked straight at Bascomb. "Holly was just drunk," he said. "All we had to do was keep out

126

of the way until he'd run out of ammunition." The unspoken accusation was in his voice.

"Sergeant, when a man takes a shot at me, drunk or sober, he had best know what he's doing," Bascomb said in a flat voice. "May I point out that he had already wounded one of the men." He holstered his pistol and turned to leave; then he added, "Holly was on the army payroll so let's get him out of here. See that he gets buried, sergeant."

With that he stalked off. Angevine stood and watched him until the man turned into a saloon. Then the sergeant sent one man after a blanket and got four others to carry Holly to the edge of town to the grave-yard. They spent an hour digging a grave for him.

There was a heavy anger in Angevine, to be burying a friend like this, with no one caring, no one seeing any value in him at all, nothing to mark the passing of a man. But the sergeant had been ordered by Bascomb to bury a body. So that's what he did. When Holly was in the ground, he told the men to cover the grave and then walked on back to the camp and sat by the fire for a long while.

It was not simply the shock of death that troubled him. He was deeply disturbed that a man could throw his life away so foolishly. Where was the judgment, the caution? Angevine himself was always cautious, always weighing the risk against the chances of getting out whole.

He had not really liked Sergeant Gore, but he had considered him a man apart, wiser than most, braver than average, yet Gore had stupidly ignored the smoke from the mountain rises. Perhaps, Angevine thought, Gore hadn't really known what the smoke meant. He should have, for he had often spoken of his experiences with the Indians. But what did it matter whether Gore knew or not? Angevine hadn't known either, yet he had been alarmed, warned, his suspicions aroused.

But Gore and the others died, threw themselves away.

And Holly, the frontier windbag, man of few accomplishments and many lies, he'd played the biggest fool of all, in Angevine's estimation. In spite of Holly's faults, Angevine had liked him, believed that they had been friends. Holly had no genuine caution, just a natural skittishness that preserved his hide because he had never been afraid to run, and then think up a couple of good reasons for it later. Holly wasn't the kind of man who played with a set bear trap, yet he had started this senseless shooting match and got himself killed because of it.

He, like Gore, just could not put aside personal prejudice, or pride or whatever it was that drove him, and do the right thing. And it suddenly dawned on Angevine that an exact analysis of the personal weaknesses of these two men was not at all important; it really didn't matter because it wouldn't have changed the outcome at all.

On the trip back, Lieutenant Bascomb, more often than not, found some reason to join Loch Angevine during the evening meal, and being a sergeant, Angevine did not object to this. He also admired Bascomb, and events he had witnessed increased that admiration. Bascomb was a leader, a man to follow, and personally, Angevine was proud to serve under him.

They talked, or rather, Angevine listened and Bascomb talked, and it came to Angevine again that in the beginning of his service he had been unable to notice much; his viewpoint had been incredibly restricted. But now, listening to Bascomb talk of his youth and his family and his years at the Academy, Angevine could think of him as another man, and at the same time still keep in proportion their differences in ability, training, and family background.

Bascomb was, by his own admission, trained from early youth to follow a military career. He was born to command and his father, a stern disciplinarian, had made sure that he rode before he could walk, had mastered the fencing foil at fourteen to bring grace and agility to the fore, and had excelled academically through private tutors.

Resin Bascomb was proud of himself, and Angevine thought that he should be, for he had had a father who guided him instead of complaining all the time. It did not matter that Angevine had posted straight A's in his mathematics; Bascomb had so dazzled his proctors that they spent long hours devising new problems to tax his mind. Listening to Bascomb, Loch Angevine realized that his grades in history were in fact puny compared to Bascomb's grasp of the subject; it had been so profound, he admitted, that he had been requested to do a definitive paper on French history. The paper, he told Angevine, had been so outstanding that an envious professor had destroyed it in a pique and thereby denied the world the illuminating experience of reading it.

Truly Resin Bascomb was an exceptional man. Angevine knew that his manner with superior officers was dignified, correct, and beyond criticism. And his handling of the troublesome Mrs. Bowen had been firm to the extreme; Angevine knew that he himself would not have spoken so.

Certainly there was not an enlisted man in the command who would not jump when Bascomb spoke, a mark of respect as well as of a sense of duty.

Loch Angevine felt that he could serve Bascomb well and at the same time do credit to himself by learning to adopt some of Bascomb's ways and thereby bring a halt to this being thrown into confusion by every adventure that came along. It just wouldn't do to go through life half panicked, recovering only in time to just barely save the situation.

A man simply had to learn to be cool-headed in this country.

A courier from Colonel Bowen found them on the second day out; he reported to Bascomb, handed him a dispatch, then stood at attention, waiting for Bascomb's reaction.

The lieutenant read it, swore a little, then laughed. "This is ridiculous," he said to no one in particular. Then he called Sergeant Angevine over. "Sergeant, this dispatch is from Colonel Bowen. Mrs. Bowen, it seems, has changed her mind about you and does not intend to travel one step further unless you are there to scout the march. Will that stupid woman's meddling never cease?" He frowned and sighed and gave other subtle vents to his annoyance. "Well, sergeant, I cannot ignore a command by a superior officer. You are relieved of your duties. Get your horse and gear and return to Tucson, and when you get there, report to Colonel Bowen immediately."

"Yes, sir." He saluted and started an about-face, then stopped. "Am I to remain with the Colonel, sir?"

"I don't know. Perhaps he will want to transfer you, since Mrs. Bowen obviously cannot rest peacefully unless she knows your eagle eye is watching over her. Confounded nonsense, that's what it is!" He waved his hand. "Be off without delay, sergeant. We'll try to struggle through without you."

His anger was mounting and Angevine could not understand it and he wasn't quite sure that he wanted to. He couldn't figure what had made Mrs. Bowen change her mind about him either. So he got his gear and his horse and left the camp, turning back toward Tucson with the messenger for company.

There wasn't much talk until Angevine dismounted to walk his horse. Then the private said, "The town's still talkin' about the gunfight, sarge."

"What is there to talk about? A drunk losing his head. And his life."

"Holly was talkin' it all over town that he was goin' to call you out, sarge. If the soldiers hadn't butted in, you'd have done him in, wouldn't you have, huh?"

"Why don't you shut your mouth?" Angevine said, and remounted.

The messenger was counting on some time on the trail, but Angevine stopped only long enough to brew some coffee and cook some pork for breakfast, and because he pushed through, they reached Tucson a little after noon on the next day.

Without bothering to wash and shave, Angevine reported to the lieutenant colonel at the hotel; Bowen seemed harried and out of sorts. He drew Angevine to one side and said, "Thank God you had the wit to get right back, sergeant. I've had a devil of a time. Mrs. Bowen is not really well and I feel it is best to humor her at times."

He droned on in a monotonous tone and Angevine listened to things no officer should inflict on an enlisted man. Bowen was a weak man, constantly debating with himself, and it made Angevine wonder how he ever got to be a colonel in the first place.

". . . of course I asked Claudia not to come," Bowen said, "but you know women, sergeant. They do not always listen to sound advice. So we must make the best of it, eh, sergeant? Peace in the family, eh?" He laughed uneasily and kept on talking, and Angevine could read the truth in the man and knew that he didn't

132

love his wife and was acutely disappointed in her and in most of the things that had happened to him. And Angevine began to understand how Bowen survived; he delegated his responsibilities, passed them all out, like prizes, and if anyone failed, then Bowen would chop their heads off and put it down in their record.

"I want you to be Mrs. Bowen's personal attendant when we reach Camp Yuma," Bowen was saying. "And on the journey back, you might reassure her that we are in no danger of hostile attack. A woman at ease is a quiet woman, eh, sergeant?"

Angevine looked at this man who had been destroyed long ago, and he thought of all the opinions he had ever had, opinions that he had held back; they were like water pressing against a dam, and the structure broke silently, yet with a force that Angevine felt to the foundation. He said, "Sir, I will escort your party to Camp Yuma because I've been ordered to. But I will not remain there as a servant of your wife. Such duty would be completely intolerable to me, sir."

"I think, sergeant, that your choice of duty is not in your hands but in mine."

"In that, sir, you are quite mistaken," Angevine said. Then, without altering his expression, he added, "An examination of my record, sir, will disclose that I am a graduate civil engineer. However, in all modesty I would like to inform you that Senator Janis, a close friend of the family, and my godfather, pressed a commission on me, but my father, who believed that every man is better for starting at the bottom, insisted that I enlist as a private." He kept looking at Bowen and watching the impression hit him, watching him mentally retreat, retrench. "If you press this, sir, I'll have to write my father and Senator Janis, who will insist that my training be better utilized."

"I-1 had no idea," Bowen said, completely routed. "Of course, sergeant, I see no need of alarming the senator over this matter."

"Thank you, sir. I was sure the colonel, once apprised of the facts, would make the correct decision."

"Yes, to be sure," Bowen said. "That will be all, sergeant. We leave in the morning."

A salute terminated the meeting and Angevine understood then the pure thrill that Holly must have known when he stood at the bar and spun his lies for drinks. The fact that Angevine was an engineer, and it was on his record gave him the springboard he needed. Senator Janis was a name he had made up on the moment, and the rest, pure claptrap, bluff, polite threat, and Bowen had bent to it.

Lying, he discovered, gave a man a sense of superiority, and he was not surprised why so many people did it.

A barber shaved him, but Angevine would not let him cut his hair; it was to his collar and in another three months he could braid it in the manner of the mountain men that Holly had always talked about. He was letting his mustache grow for it was a luxu-

134

rious red, as was his hair.

A bath refreshed him and took away a certain gaminess that had been following him around, and afterward he went to the stable to sleep in the haystack. It was nightfall when he woke and the noise of the town was a clamor along the main front. A horseman came into the stable and put up his horse, looked at Angevine curiously, but said nothing.

A small Mexican restaurant sold him a bowl of chili beans for a dime, and when that failed to fill him, he bought three *tacos* and washed it all down with strong coffee. On the street again, he saw three soldiers farther down, cheering on a fourth who was brawling with two civilians. It was an unfair contest, Angevine thought, and he walked down there and butted right into it, catching one man by the collar and spinning him away. When the man started to bore in, Angevine lifted the muzzle of the Henry rifle and said, "One at a time."

He recognized the man as the rider who had come into the stable to put up his horse, and he held him off while the soldier battered the other man down. The soldier, having won, decided not to push his luck and turned with his friends into the cantina and the crowd stayed in the street, waiting to see what the Indian-fighter and the stranger were going to do.

Angevine said, "You want to go into the cantina and start something, then go right ahead." The beaten man was getting to his hands and knees and finally he made his feet and staggered off down the street.

The stranger watched him go, then shook his head.

135

"I can't stand a man who butts in." He looked carefully at Angevine and saw the army pants and boots and he frowned because the buckskin jacket and Mexican hat confused him. "You army, mister?"

"Sergeant Angevine. I don't know you."

"Name's Collins. I trade with the Injuns. The Pimas." He was a tall, heavily armed man with a brace of pistols and a long knife at his belt. "I'll let this go this time, sergeant."

"I don't care if you do or not," Angevine said. "Next time you fight a soldier, keep your friends out of it."

"I'll try to remember," Collins said. "Was you to be around Camp Yuma, I'd—"

"You can find me there," Angevine said. He turned his head and looked at the people gathered around. "Don't you people have anything to do?"

It was a mild question, mildly put, but they had no argument in mind and within a minute Collins and Angevine stood alone in the street.

Collins said, "You did that easy enough, sergeant. Got a bit of a reputation, huh?" He laughed softly. "Well, I guess this turned out all right for me. Hate to make anything of a man until I get to know him a little. You ridin' with the colonel in the mornin'?"

"That's right."

"Ah, you're the guide the woman set up such a howl about. Should have known." He nodded his head. "Big Injun-fighter, I hear. Shot up Holly too, I hear. I'd like to do some business with the 'Paches if I had an in with 'em."

"Whisky and guns?"

Collins laughed again. "Sergeant, you'd have to catch me to prove it, and you ain't about to do that. But you've got to figure it this way: if the 'Paches had guns and ammo, they wouldn't have to kill to steal it, would they?" He touched the brim of his hat with his fingers. "I'll see you around, huh?"

"Don't go out of your way," Angevine said, and stood there, watching the first man he had ever hated on sight walk away.

9

Sergeant Angevine did not enjoy the six-day march to Yuma, for Colonel Bowen poked along, catered to his wife's whims, and let her boss the soldiers. Angevine tried to stand clear of the whole thing by simply remaining away from the camp as much as possible. He would roll out early and scout the camp long before Mrs. Bowen woke with her new complaints for the day, and in the evening, he would remain away until dark and thereby avoid her.

She could not complain because he was scouting.

During the trip, Angevine observed Eleanor Bowen, a very nice girl who was getting impatient to do things on her own and think thoughts of her own. Angevine believed that she'd break away from her mother if the right man came along.

When they crossed the desert, they cut northward to

the Gila River and followed it on into Camp Yuma, perched on a rocky rise in the most forbidding land Angevine had ever seen. Mrs. Bowen and Eleanor went immediately to the Colonel's adobe, and Angevine took his jaded horse to the stable, saddled a fresh one, drew supplies, and was away from the post well before sunset.

That night he camped along the river with no fire. He was amused at the way he got out of there before Colonel Bowen could give him any more orders and detain him further. Angevine did not want to serve with Bowen because the major was not going anywhere or doing anything; there was nothing to be learned from the man. He was not brave. He was not even smart. And Angevine did not want to be with a man who was set apart by weakness; he knew what that was from personal experience and wanted no more of it. He would not learn to know men, to understand life, from Major Bowen, for the man was not living life; he was gliding through it, like a canoe adrift, making a silent passage of it and hoping that no force upset him.

Angevine thought about his father and what they had talked about before he left home; he had wondered then what he sought and had been told that he would recognize it. He was not sure that he did, but he knew now what he did not seek, which he thought was some progress.

Gore had disappointed him, and Holly had come to nothing. Now he wanted to get back to Lieutenant

Bascomb, feeling certain that after two false starts, this was the man to watch, the man to be with, the man who had already traveled the splendid road to manhood.

Three days out of Yuma, Angevine came across a set of northbound tracks and he paused to study them. A rider had passed this way with two pack horses and since some of the tracks were so much deeper, his attention was drawn to them and he wondered who could be passing this way, for there was nothing to the north but Pima Indians and more desert.

He would have paid little attention to the tracks except that the pack horses had obviously been heavily loaded, and it made him wonder what anyone was doing in this vast, lonesome desert with pack horses. He knew nothing of mining, except what he had gleaned from textbooks, but he was certain that no ore existed in the desert.

So the man wasn't a prospector.

A trader? He thought about it and remembered Collins, and dislike and mistrust bloomed in his mind. He swung north and followed the tracks. An hour later he swam the river and picked up the tracks on the other side and kept at it the rest of that day, moving through this desert with the tawny sand and the glare hurting his eyes and the buttes rising like stone cathedrals in the distance.

This was a seemingly lifeless country, yet he was not fooled by it, for he had learned that one need not constantly stir up a cloud of dust in order to be active.

Before dark he saw some dense trees in the distance and knew that he was heading for a spring, but he did not recklessly plunge headlong toward it. Instead he picketed his horse several miles away and went the rest of the way on foot, moving easily and taking care that he would not be seen.

He tried to imitate the Apaches. When he reached the spring he found Collins camped there, his pack horses picketed in the dense cover. Collins had a very small fire going and was making coffee, and when Loch Angevine thought about that, he realized that Collins was expecting someone, or he wouldn't have had the fire.

Angevine worked close, to within twenty yards, then said, "We meet sooner than I expected, Collins."

The man's reaction was like a bound spring released; he jumped and drew his pistol and whirled and fired, but a split second behind Angevine's shot. The .44 bullet caught Collins in the breastbone and staggered him and he tried to raise his pistol for another shot, but the life ran out of him and he fell soddenly.

Angevine's shot had been a reaction for he had been surprised by Collins' sudden move, yet he retained his presence of mind and knew that he couldn't hang around. That shot had bounded around the country and had surely been heard by someone, if only the person Collins had been waiting to see.

So he took Coffins' pistols, then went to his pack horses, had his look, and found rifles; he had expected something like that. Then he looked back at the dead man and said softly, "Well, I caught you quicker than you thought, didn't I?"

Mounting Collins' horse and leading the pack animals, Angevine went back to where he had left his own horse; then he started toward the river, moving as rapidly as he dared through the darkness.

When he reached the river, he had lost all track of time, but it didn't matter now; he crossed and set a direction that would eventually take him to Tucson, and he moved as rapidly as he could, keeping in mind that he had a long way to go and couldn't kill the horses.

By sleeping when he could and making cold camp, Angevine returned to Tucson in four days, and he set up camp in the plaza, which irritated some of the merchants, at least until they found out what Collins had been selling.

Public feeling ran high and had Collins been alive they would have hung him, for they had all had their troubles with the Apaches and no one was so dense that he failed to see how the Apaches got firearms and ammunition; Collins traded with the Pimas, who traded with the Apaches.

Two civilians volunteered to ride east and locate the telegraph camp, and they carried Angevine's message to Lieutenant Bascomb. Several other civilians took turns helping Angevine guard the rifles; he remained in the plaza and it became quite a thing, him camped there and the women in town bringing him food every day.

There was no danger of anyone stealing the rifles, for Angevine had taken some out of the pack and stacked them in a military manner. People never tired of coming and looking at them and talking about how those rifles would never kill a settler and how there was the man who had saved them all.

Finally Bascomb and a detail arrived and the cavalry major was with him; the army immediately took charge of the rifles, inventoried them, and rented a building to lock them in. The cavalry major acted as though Angevine's vigil had been truly heroic, another Horatius at the bridge.

After being relieved of duty, Angevine had a bath and a shave, then was asked to come to the hotel where the major had established a sort of headquarters.

Lieutenant Bascomb was there, smoking a cigar and smiling; after all, he had trained Angevine, instilled in him this superb sense of duty. The major was very friendly; he offered Angevine a cigar and a drink, and since he could not refuse both without offending, Angevine took the drink then sat for a few minutes with a good fire in his belly.

"Sergeant, your action was most distinguished. Most distinguished," the major said and rocked on his heels as though he were pleased with Providence for sending him soldiers of this caliber. He acted as though, with some additional effort, Angevine might be good enough to be a cavalryman.

The cavalry major had some plans forming in his

mind and he saw no reason to wait and consult the infantry major about them and share mention in the report. So he drew a chair around and faced Sergeant Angevine and said, "It occurs to me, sergeant, that here is a golden opportunity. We mustn't let it slip through our fingers." He glanced at Lieutenant Bascomb. "Don't you agree?"

"Indeed I do, sir," Bascomb said quickly and wondered what he was agreeing to.

"We have the rifles and we know the Indians Collins dealt with. I've had my eye on that man for a long time, sergeant." He glanced again at Bascomb, who seemed surprised. "I feigned ignorance, Mr. Bascomb, because when the couriers reported to me I didn't want anyone else to suspect the extent of my knowledge." He turned back to Angevine. "I want you to take those rifles back and sell them to the Pimas. Learn all you can so that we can run down the source of these arms."

"They are of Spanish manufacture, sir," Bascomb put in.

The major became irritated. "Mr. Bascomb, just because the crow roosts in the peach tree does not indicate that he has not dined in the cornfield." He looked hard at him, as if to tell him that if he didn't have intelligent remarks to make, it would be better if he kept still. "Now, sergeant, we'll get you fresh horses and you can be on your way. I want you to stay with the Pimas after you make the sale. Meet their Apache contacts and report back to me with full information. Is that clear?"

"Yes, sir, but it would be better to find someone who can speak——"

Bascomb interrupted. "Damn it, Angevine, let's have none of your infernal modesty!"

"The sergeant understands that I want results," the major said. "Success is based on results, not failure. Dismissed, sergeant."

Angevine left, and when he stopped on the hotel porch, his temper got away from him for a moment and he flung his hat to the planks, then self-consciously picked it up and clapped it on his head and walked on down the street.

He was hard put not to call the major a fool, for Angevine could not see any benefit in making Indian contact and selling the rifles. Angevine felt certain that Collins bought them in Mexico, and the Apaches frequently made forays into that territory themselves. If the Indians had known where Collins had been getting them, they wouldn't have had to deal with him in the first place.

It wasn't hard to figure out that Collins had the rifles buried somewhere while he'd been in Tucson. He'd left about the same time as the Bowen party, so it just had to be that the rifles had been cached.

No one, Angevine reasoned, would know that Collins was dead. In Mexico they wouldn't know it, and an idea formed carefully and he thought over the details of it, then made up his mind.

He wrote a note to the major, then got Collins' horse

and the pack horses and had the rifles loaded. He drew rations, delivered the note to the hotel clerk, and cleared town a little after midnight, quietly enough not to attract attention.

For an hour he moved west, then cut south, heading toward Mexico, a distance of some one hundred miles.

Come dawn he was deep into the mountains, and since he estimated that somewhere in this area Collins had buried the rifles, Angevine searched out a place and got rid of his load on the pack horses.

Then he made a dry camp and rested for several hours while the heat of the day began to build.

In the hotel, the cavalry major was awake and dressing, and Lieutenant Bascomb knocked and stepped inside, bearing Angevine's message. "For you, sir," Bascomb said, handing it over.

The major read it:

Major Hoskins:
So enthused over your brilliant plan, am unable to
wait. Leaving immediately.

L. Angevine, Sgt., Eng.

"By God, that's what I call a real soldier," the major said. "Won't you join me in breakfast, Bascomb?"

Traveling in broad daylight through Apache country was not Angevine's notion of relaxation, but he had learned that if a man remained alert and well armed, he would not be rashly attacked by the Apaches. They were very brave, but they did not like to lose many of their warriors. In his encounters with them he had noticed that they did not attack in great numbers, and he began to think that there weren't too many of them to begin with. Perhaps, he reasoned, that was why they always broke off when two or three were killed; the game was just not worth the risk.

It was a theory that he meant to investigate.

He did not once think that he passed through the country unnoticed; he was certain that he was being watched constantly, but he remained alert and kept his repeating rifle in his hands and pistols ready at his belt, for he had the two he had taken off Collins. His own service revolver hung on the saddle.

When he had killed Collins, Angevine took the man's handguns for two reasons: he didn't want them to fall into the hands of the Indians and Collins had had the revolvers converted to take the .44 Henry cartridge, which made them better than Angevine's own service pistol, which loaded with cap and ball paper cartridges.

No authority on weapons, Angevine still was aware of the importance they played on the frontier, and after the fight at the spring he had noticed that the Apaches carried carbines and rifles of good quality. Generally they were Confederate military or late model arms taken off fallen soldiers.

Apaches, he believed, raided for weapons and horses, not for food or for knicknacks and money. The Apaches prized weapons, regarded them highly, and knew how to use them.

All of which put Collins in a very profitable business.

Through the day Angevine's compass guided him, and that night, the stars, and he did not make a camp but dozed in the saddle and kept moving, giving the Apaches no chance to jump him. The night was clear and his visibility was good and he moved southward toward a clearly defined pass, crested it at dawn, and with his glass could make out a small Mexican village some miles beyond.

In three hours he came within range of yapping dogs who ran out to meet him and worry the horses. The village was a cluster of adobe huts and narrow streets and a grove of trees marked the plaza and the central well.

By his estimate the village contained three hundred people. Mostly they were poor, although at the west edge of town a large hacienda nestled in luxury behind a high wall. It was, Angevine thought, like all places, neither all poor nor all rich, for wealth had a way of flowing away from most and toward a few; it was a law of nature, seemingly, and man couldn't do much to stop it.

He dismounted in the square and tied the horses, then went into the cantina, a squat adobe that was cool and dim inside. The man in charge spoke no English and Angevine spoke no Spanish, so he just made a drinking motion and the man poured into a glass.

One was enough; it felt as though he had swallowed

hot wax. Angevine paid him and went out and stood under the shade trees for a time, looking around the town; there wasn't anything that couldn't be seen in five minutes.

There was an inn across the plaza, and a harness maker next to it. There was a store farther down, while to Angevine's left, a restaurant and bakery filled the air with pleasant aromas. He went there because he hadn't had hot food for nearly two days. Several women worked hard rolling dough and frying cakes. He bought what he wanted, sat down just outside the door, and ate.

Everyone in the village had their look at him and at the horses he rode, which they knew belonged to Collins; at least Angevine hoped that they were recognized because he believed that this was where Collins had spent a lot of his time.

Angevine discovered siesta time; during the bad heat of the day it seemed that everyone died—it was that quiet. Even the dogs and children were silent, and he sat in the shade and slept because that was what everyone else did.

Much later in the afternoon, when the sun started to slant down, the village came alive again and the women gathered at the plaza and pounded their washing with sticks and the dogs yapped about and naked children chased each other.

Angevine put up his horses at the stable and slept there the first night, and the next day he did nothing but sleep and roam around. When he got hungry, he always went to the restaurant, and when he was tired, he parked under a tree.

No one spoke to him or bothered him and on the third day his patience was beginning to grow a little thin and he began to think that he had made a bad guess. Still he felt that everyone recognized Collins' horses and for that reason he decided to stay on.

He bought a Mexican *serape* and a pair of musical spurs, and since his boots were playing out, he had the shoemaker work on a pair with high square tops and considerable hand-tooling.

He had been in the village a little over a week when three wagons arrived and he could see that the drivers were Americans; they were bluff and noisy and they all went into the cantina and stayed a while.

Then one of them came out and looked up and down the street, but Angevine felt certain that this was a cover so the man could look him over. Since arriving, Angevine had taken to leaving his rifle hidden in the stable loft, but under the *serape* he wore his pistols, and when the teamster started walking toward him, Angevine slipped one free of the holster, cocked it, and held it in his lap under the *serape.*

The man grinned through his beard when he came up. "Hear you're an American," he said, breaking out a cigar and a match. "I get down this way every month or so. Do some tradin'. Leather goods, hides, some silver, and these Mexicans make some cakes and things that keep right well. Good market in Tucson." He puffed on his cigar. "What's your line?"

149

"Not asking questions," Angevine said.

The man laughed. "Americans are hard to come by down here. You ought to try hard to be friendly." He studied Angevine through eyes pulled into puffy slits. "Seems I recall you from somewhere. Ain't I seen you around Tucson?"

"I've been there."

"Sure, I remember you. You're the Apache fighter." He took his cigar out of his mouth. "A soldier, by God!" His manner turned hard and he reached to his belt and put his hand around the butt of his pistol. "What the hell you doin' with Collins' horses? Where's Collins?"

"Dead," Angevine said. "And you're going to be if you don't take your hand away from your pistol." He waited for a heartbeat, then flicked aside the *serape* and let the teamster take a look down the bore of the Remington. "Collins was an unreasonable man. I only wanted half of his business. A sergeant's pay isn't much. But he couldn't see it, so now I've got it all."

The teamster scratched his beard and let go of the notion of drawing his revolver. "You haven't got much, soldier. Collins had help."

"I'll get what I need."

"Not unless we say so," the man said. "You wait here."

"I wasn't going anywhere," Angevine told him, and watched him walk back to the cantina.

He wasn't a bit fooled because the teamster had backed down, and that evening he moved to another place in the stable. He found some boards, laid them across two of the highest rafters, climbed up there, and waited, because he expected visitors.

For a time it seemed that he was mistaken, for midnight came and went and no one came into the stable. He slept in bits and pieces and then in the late hours he woke to a slight sound outside and reached for his pistols which he had cocked and laid in front of him on the boards.

There was just enough light to make out the stable archway, and two men came in very quietly and carefully mounted the ladder to the loft. One of them crouched down and moved into the hay where Angevine had been sleeping and the other remained on the top of the ladder, a pistol in his hand.

Then Angevine said, "Up here," and immediately drew fire. One bullet whined by and the other man fired into the planks. Then Angevine shot the man off the ladder and listened to him fall. The other man fired again but the planks kept the bullet from reaching Angevine; he pointed down, fired at the last muzzle flash and heard the man grunt heavily and stumble as he moved to the ladder. He reached it, started down, then the strength left him, and he fell soddenly.

Angevine watched him crawl toward the stable door, but he never made it. Getting down from his high perch, Angevine holstered his pistols and went down the ladder.

The first man was dead and it made Angevine feel uneasy to look at the damage his bullet had done.

Then he walked over to the other man and rolled him over. He was still alive and he reached for Angevine's leg, gripped it feebly for a moment, then fell back, dead.

Going to the stable door, Angevine had a look in all directions, but he saw no one; they were behind their walls, letting the *Americanos* settle their own troubles, and he supposed this was really the best way after all.

He found some candles in a box and put a match to one so he could see more clearly the faces of the two men. They were, as he had thought all along, two of the teamsters who had come to the village with the wagons.

So he blew out the candle, got his blankets, went over to the plaza, and slept out the rest of the night by the well curbing, telling himself that the difference between a man living and dying was just a matter of caution.

He wondered how he could feel no remorse for having shot two men, and he knew it wasn't because he was defending himself; there were many ways a man could do that without taking a life. Then he supposed that he was changing, beginning to judge other men and to decide in his own mind whether or not they were to live or die, whether they were good or bad. He knew that he had been prepared to shoot Collins when he approached the man's fire, and when Collins whirled around, Angevine had already set himself to shoot.

He supposed that his father would say that this was

the brave thing to do, the right thing, but he knew it wasn't. It was some animal law that everyone obeyed and no one forgot, even for a moment, and the man who lapsed could and often did get killed.

Angevine had to make sure he wasn't the one who died.

10

Señor Juan Ortega lived in the fine house behind the fine, high wall and he journeyed forth only upon rare occasions, and then he rode in a splendid buggy drawn by a pair of splendid horses and driven by a peon who shared one idea with his master: neither felt that he had enough money. The peon had only a few pesos, hardly enough to feed his family and Ortega had thousands of pesos, yet not enough to make him feel that even more would not be better.

When dawn came, the Mexicans went to the stable to see the dead men and the surviving teamster rode out of town toward the Ortega hacienda. An hour later, Ortega came to town in his buggy and waited for Loch Angevine in the plaza.

Angevine was having his morning meal of corn cakes, coffee, and pork; he came out of the small adobe, saw Ortega sitting in his rig, then walked over.

The Mexican was fifty-some, very slender, almost delicate; he had a thin face and a good mustache and dark, expressionless eyes. He smiled as Angevine stopped by the off wheel, and said, "Señor, you have caused me great inconvenience. In addition, it will cost me two pesos to have them buried."

"We all have to pay for our mistakes," Angevine said. "Did you really think I was fooled into falling asleep?" He shook his head. "You've got three wagons and cargo and only one man left to drive them."

"You are a soldier of the *Estados Unidos*," Ortega said. "I could not trust you."

"Now you don't have any choice," Angevine told him. "You've got to ask yourself what I'd be doing down here if I was still in the army. A sergeant's pay isn't much, so I decided to get out when I had the chance. Collins wouldn't talk business, so I shot him, took his horses, and rode south."

"Where are the guns?"

"Hid. They're safe until I'm ready."

Ortega motioned for Angevine to get into the buggy. "Please accept the hospitality of my house, señor. We can discuss details and arrangements in comfort."

Angevine thought about it a moment, nodded, then got into the buggy; it was an open brougham and he sat across from Ortega, his *serape* pushed aside so that both his pistols were exposed.

"You are very careful," Ortega remarked, then smiled.

"It keeps me alive."

There was no more talk and they drove on to the hacienda. The gates were opened, they passed inside, and the gates were closed again, and Angevine realized that getting out might be more of a problem than getting in.

Chickens scattered as they wheeled across the yard and pulled up by the shaded veranda. Angevine got down and a peon hurried to give Ortega a hand, then the remaining teamster stepped out and stood by the door. It was the same man who had once spoken to Angevine and he seemed very unhappy.

Angevine said, "I'll bet you miss your friends already, huh?"

"Where are the rifles?" the teamster asked.

Ortega waved his hand. "There is time to discuss it later. Come inside, please."

They went into a large study and a servant brought them coffee. Angevine took a chair that was placed so he could see the door and still watch both of them. He could not describe the sensation of deliberately walking into this danger and he realized that he had never done this before, never actually placed himself in danger by his own volition.

Before, fate had shoved him, circumstance had moved him, or danger had brushed him, forcing him to act, and he supposed that this was the reason he never felt particularly brave about it afterward.

But this was different. This was what his father had talked about, and it pleased him to finally find out, to understand, and not to fall weakly in a faint.

Ortega lit a cigar and walked up and down and Angevine watched him. The teamster kept rubbing his hands against the legs of his pants and finally he said,

"You tell me what the hell we're going to do, Ortega."

"We are going to think." He stopped walking and leaned against a heavy table. "Soldier, I should thank you for pointing out the weakness of our little venture. With two men gone, we are seriously handicapped." He smiled pleasantly. "And you have the rifles that Collins was to sell."

"Yeah, let's start with the rifles," the teamster said. "Where are they, soldier?"

"Safe," Angevine said. "That's all you need to know."

"We will get the rifles in due time," Ortega said. "Soldier, what is it you want? You have gone to much trouble, coming here this way."

"I think it's foolish to sell to the Pimas when you can sell to the Apaches," Angevine said.

The teamster laughed and Ortega shook his head. "For years, the Mexican government has paid rewards for Apaches. We would be killed before we could tell them what we wanted."

"I wouldn't," Angevine said easily. "I've talked to Coloradas. I could do business with them."

Ortega didn't believe it, but the teamster was inclined to. "He may have something there," he said. "No, I've heard talk about this pistol. He came up like a dust devil and he's made a lot of smoke. A fella I knew was in Silver City when he came ridin' in with some dead Apaches, and you know you just don't *see* dead Apaches. And it's no damned secret that he got through the pass a couple of times and fought the

156

Apaches to a draw." He bobbed his head. "I'd listen, Ortega. He reads their smoke, I hear tell, and talks the lingo."

Angevine's presence of mind kept him from showing surprise, and he wondered how that fantastic story ever got around; he supposed that everyone who repeated it added just a little to it. Still he wasn't going to call the teamster a liar, and even Ortega seemed impressed.

"I have never known a man," he said, "who could deal with the Apaches."

"You're looking at one," Angevine said casually. "Ortega, don't you think that the Apaches would rather buy guns than steal them one at a time? If you're not interested, I have guns to sell."

"But you are not free to sell them," Ortega pointed out. "You are my—ah, guest."

"I'd shoot my way out of here if I had to."

"But you would never live to cross the yard."

"Maybe, but you'd never live to see me fall either."

To sit here and bargain with lives was a new experience and he could see that neither the teamster nor Ortega took him lightly. The Mexican said, "The point is well taken. After all, Carney and Rice are dead, and they were experienced men. But how do we settle this?"

"I'll go back, get the rifles and make the sale to the Apaches," Angevine said. "You have another load ready to bring across the border."

"How do we know you won't sell the rifles and skip

with the money?" the teamster wanted to know.

"If I did that I'd cut off my source of supply, wouldn't I?" He pointed his finger. "You're stupid. Don't do any of the thinking, huh?" His glance swung to Ortega. "I'll take half. The rest is yours to split however you like."

The Mexican frowned. "Collins only got a quarter."

"Collins wasn't dealing with the Apaches either. Without the Pimas in on it, the profit will be higher. Besides, what choice do you have?"

Ortega shrugged. "The price might be so high that I would consider it cheaper to kill you and sacrifice the rifles Collins had and start all over."

"A hundred rifles worth fifty dollars apiece to an Indian?" Loch Angevine shook his head. "You would never throw that kind of money away, and I know it." He stood up and kept one hand under his *serape*. "In thirty days I'll be looking for you somewhere south of Tucson. Have another wagon load for me."

"You're not leaving us?" Ortega asked, surprised.

Angevine stopped at the door. "My business is finished. Our deal is set. Have a horse brought around for me. I'll be leaving the village within an hour."

"Alone?"

"That's the way I want it. It's either that or no rifles." He looked at the teamster. "The Apaches won't catch me on my way back, and neither will you if you try to follow me. But I'll make sure I see you and I'll leave you out there for the buzzards to pick clean. Now will you tell your servant to fetch the horse?"

Ortega summoned a man and there was some delay and they waited on the porch for the horse to be brought around. Angevine mounted and still kept one hand under his *serape*. "Walk with me to the gate, Ortega."

"You do not trust me," Ortega said.

"That's very perceptive of you," Angevine said and turned the horse in such a way that Ortega had to move or be shouldered off his feet. They walked slowly to the gate and it was opened at Ortega's command. "Perhaps a hundred and fifty yards farther. A command, a rifle shot—" He smiled and left the obvious unsaid.

"You are very careful, soldier."

"Yes, I stay alive that way."

When they reached a point where Angevine felt it was safe, he spurred the horse and rode rapidly back to the village. It took him fifteen minutes to gather his gear and get the pack horses and clear out. Once free of the village, he rode north for several miles and moved up into the high rocks and made camp. With his glass he studied the back trail, and just before dark he was rewarded with a spiral of dust that marked the passage of a single rider.

The teamster was trailing him, as Angevine expected him to.

Picketing the horses, he worked his way down off the mountain flank and moved back along the trail to a narrow place and hunkered down to wait. The daylight was fading rapidly and he guessed not more than a half hour remained.

With an ear to the ground he heard the rider approach, and Angevine carefully worked the lever of his rifle, closing it gently so as not to make any sound. Then the horseman came up the rise; he was looking down, trying to follow the tracks in the failing light, and because he was concentrating so hard, he failed to see Angevine until it was too late.

The man made a half motion toward his pistol, then stopped when Angevine shouldered the rifle. "It'll make a noise, but that won't stop me," Angevine said. "Drop your weapons!"

The teamster disarmed himself, swearing softly while he did so, and Angevine gathered up pistol and rifle, smashed them to uselessness against a rock, then tied the man to the saddle, hand and foot.

"We've got a long ride ahead of us, friend. If you hadn't been so damned stubborn and foolish you wouldn't be making it."

"Where we goin'?"

"You'll see," Angevine said and led the man up the rocks to where the horses were tied.

Lieutenant Bascomb was stationed with a detail of soldiers in Tucson when Sergeant Angevine returned with his prisoner, and after turning the man over to a military guard, Angevine made his report.

It was difficult for Bascomb to decide whether he should give Angevine a court-martial or write him up in a dispatch; he had disregarded orders completely

160

and taken off in the wrong direction, but he had come back with success in his pocket, and you could hardly rack a man for that.

Bascomb immediately telegraphed the major, who promised to arrive in four days from Camp Yuma with two companies of cavalry, and since the major made no issue of Angevine's disobedience, Bascomb said nothing.

He was willing to forget it if the major was.

Angevine got a bath and a shave, which made him seem somewhat less than a wild man, and Bascomb detailed him as an assistant, feeling that with any luck Angevine would do something else to distinguish himself and by sticking close some of it might rub off.

It seemed strange to Bascomb that this once seemingly timid, correct soldier could, in the space of six months, transform himself into a full-blown Indian-fighter. And the more Bascomb thought about it, the more convinced he became that Angevine's past contained some pretty lurid events which he wished hidden. Bascomb remembered questioning Angevine once and recalled that the answers had been unsatisfactory then, and now he felt more strongly that his first hunch had been right.

He knew the kind, like a flash in the pan, quickly making their mark and just as quickly passing on, either killed in some violent interlude or moving on to some wilder adventure.

Yet Bascomb saw clearly that an officer who handled the Loch Angevines of the world understandingly would soon cover himself with distinction; these men sought trouble like a magnet in a keg of nails, and a junior officer rarely encountered the kind of situation in peacetime which might cause rapid promotion.

Therefore, in spite of training, instincts, and military regulations, Resin Bascomb induced Angevine to share a room with him at the hotel, and in the confines of the four walls, the lieutenant expressed his impatience with waiting for the major to arrive. He could, by wiring the base camp, have twelve more men in town by tomorrow noon, which would give him a force of twenty-three.

With Angevine as scout, they could go south and raid Ortega's *rancho,* destroy or return with the illegal guns, and lay the whole thing like a grand package at the major's feet.

Bascomb had convinced himself that this bold action would assist his elevation to captain.

Angevine thought that Ortega's place was too well fortified and they would meet with disaster. Besides, he pointed out, they were taking an armed military force into another country and he didn't think that could be done. Bascomb pointed out that Ortega's place was a running sore. Destroying one cache of arms was nothing. The source had to be wiped out. Surprise was on their side and speed was of the essence. Angevine recognized that there was no arguing with a superior officer who might, at that, be right.

Sergeant Angevine was placed in charge of mounts

and supplies, and by noon the next day, Bascomb had his command assembled and ready to mount. They left Tucson with a lot of ceremony and they turned south. Before nightfall the soldiers, unaccustomed to riding, were feeling saddle galled and they had to make camp early. Bascomb, ignoring the foolishness of a fire, posted heavy guards, which kept most of the soldiers on their feet most of the night, and for the sake of hot coffee they made a weary march of it the next day.

When they reached the border, Angevine stopped, reminding Bascomb that he was defying regulations to cross it.

Bascomb surveyed the country around for a moment, then said, "Sergeant, I see no indication that this is the border. I am positive it is thirty miles farther."

"Sir, I tell you—"

"Thank you, but I do not need to be told anything. How far is the village and hacienda?"

"Eight miles."

"We'll camp here then and wait until the dark hours before dawn."

"Sir, hadn't you better look it over first?"

"Nonsense. You've given me a detailed description." He dismounted stiffly, as a man will when he finds riding a chore and, as a consequence, does little of it. "Sergeant, I will take the main force and breach the main gate. You take a party of five and scale the walls."

"Sir, the only reason Ortega's place still stands is

because he's built it strong enough to hold out the Apaches. I just wouldn't hit that gate square on. It's four inch oak."

"You idiot, do you expect me to huff and blow it down? Scale that wall, kill off the guards at the gate, and throw the bar." He clamped his lips tightly together as though he were determined to explain nothing further. "Sergeant, I want no more argument. Now get some rest, for I'm relying heavily on you when we go in."

"Yes, sir." He started to turn away, then said, "Lieutenant, I guess you're remembering that Ortega will be on the lookout for trouble since his man didn't come back."

"I believe we can overcome that factor, sergeant. Damn it, I am committed to a course of action and I mean to follow it. By now the major has already reached Tucson and if I came back without a sweeping success—" He closed that off and stood there considering the dismal possibilities of it. "Carry on, sergeant, and don't fail me."

"If it's possible to get over that wall, sir, we'll do it, but I'd still send the men in afoot."

"How's that, sergeant? What are you talking about?"

"Well, sir, I've been trying to get you to listen. I've been inside there and Ortega's men have only single shot muskets, sir. So I'd dismount and drive the horses in toward the wall. They'll fire and your men can rush them in the dust and confusion. Besides, it might give us enough of a diversion to get over the wall."

164

Bascomb pulled his lip. "That does have some merit. I'll consider it."

Before he stretched out to rest, Angevine picked the men he wanted with him when he went over the wall; he selected men who had been along with Mrs. Bowen's escort, men who had been under fire and had not broken. It struck him then that he was looking for bravery, the way his father and his brothers had looked to him and had not found it.

But it wasn't bravery at all, Angevine discovered. It was competence, the ability to do and do well and not consider too strongly the odds. He did not ask these men to do this without fear, or without complaint, or objection; he simply asked them to do it, and they would because it was asked of them.

They didn't shrink and it wasn't too important that what they did was right, or even totally necessary. It was a part of their life and they would live it.

He slept soundly because he had no guard duty, and when the predawn wind blew chilly, they all got up and made ready and walked their horses down the last slope toward the hacienda. The village lay to their left and Angevine, with his detail, left the main body. With their horses and with ropes coiled over their arms, the little group made for the west wall.

When they drew near the wall, Angevine tied a rope through the trigger guard of a spare pistol, tossed it up twice before having it go around the limb of an overhanging tree. Then he pulled the rope down and two men held it taut while he climbed up, made the branch, and then pulled up a rope ladder they had fashioned.

To make room for the others, he climbed along the limb until he was right over the broad wall, and he peered around carefully and saw one man dozing at his post farther down.

Removing his spurs, Angevine dropped down to the wall while the others crouched amid the foliage of the tree. Soundlessly he made his way along, bent over to show less of himself. The guard was no more than six yards away, head bent forward, sleeping soundly against orders.

A knife deep in the back would do the job, but Angevine found that he just couldn't kill this man, so he reversed the knife and crept forward. When he struck, he put his strength into it and knocked the man out, catching him before he could keel over.

Sheathing his knife, Angevine grabbed the Mexican's arms, lowered him as far as he could along the outside of the wall, then dropped him and heard him land.

He didn't think the ten foot drop had really hurt him any.

The others came up behind him, belly down atop the wall and they looked around. There was some movement in the yard, near the house, and they counted four guards on duty there.

The arch of the gate blocked out their view ahead of them, but Angevine felt sure that another guard walked atop the wall, or slept. Either way, he was

166

there and they couldn't take care of him without attracting attention.

He motioned for the rope to be passed up and he uncoiled it, letting it drape down inside the wall. The free end was made fast around the arch of the gate, and he dropped over, quickly letting himself down.

His feet had hardly touched the ground when Bascomb started the horses down and they made a drumming din that brought everyone in the hacienda wide awake. One of the guards by the house fired his musket, and from a building on the far side, a dozen men started dashing toward the wall.

Two others dropped down off the rope and Angevine motioned for them to get to the gate and shoot the bar. He knelt and shouldered his repeater and began to fire, keeping up a steady run of it and not really caring whether or not he hit anyone.

The rest of his detail was down and two knelt beside him and began shooting while the others forced back the bar and got the main gate open.

The Mexicans were not coming on, but falling back and taking cover and this surprised Angevine and worried him, for they should have kept up their charge and overrun them. Then above the shouting he heard a new sound, a creaking of unoiled wheels, and it was a moment before he knew what it was.

"Cannon!" he shouted. "Through the gate! Through the gate!"

He rushed the open gate, determined to get through and stop Bascomb who would be rushing up with his men under cover of the dust raised by the horses.

But he was too late for the cannon boomed from somewhere near the veranda and grape shot tore through the main gate opening and caught Bascomb and his men just as they breached it.

One moment they were bowling through and the next they were being flung like dolls. Then a second cannon belched and more shot splattered the framework of the gate.

Angevine was not sure how many had been killed or wounded; there was no time to tell. He saw Bascomb writhing on the ground, flapping the stump of one arm and bleeding horribly from a head wound.

"Fall back! Fall back!" Angevine shouted and somehow above the screaming and confusion this order was heard and they rushed away from the gate, taking some of the wounded and leaving the dead. Angevine got hold of Bascomb. The man was raving, out of his head, but Angevine managed to drag him back away from the wall.

Someone had been gathering the horses and these were brought up; not all of them had been caught, but by a quick count, Bascomb had lost twelve men, so there were enough horses. They mounted and rode out, racing back away from the wall to be out of any rifle fire; it was a complete rout, an utterly disorganized and undignified retreat.

They ran.

Angevine got Bascomb to the foot of the pass, and he built a large fire there and it attracted the others and they came drifting in, in pairs, some alone, but all sick and ashamed and knowing they couldn't do anything about it because it was all wrong.

"We'll go back now," Angevine told them.

Lieutenant Bascomb was still alive, barely, and he had one lucid moment before he died, for he looked at Angevine and said, "I'm sorry."

The Mexicans did not pursue; there was no reason to.

Angevine insisted they pile rocks over Bascomb; none of them liked to do this, to waste the time, but he told them to and they did it. Then he had the survivors mount, the well and the wounded, motioned them into march order, and turned them north.

11

Leading what was left of Bascomb's command back across the border, Sergeant Angevine had difficulty understanding that Bascomb was really dead. But he knew he was, for his own uniform was matted and spotted with Bascomb's blood, and he had stretched Bascomb out on the ground and watched him die.

No one could have saved him; Angevine knew that. Not with an arm gone and his skull laid open and one whole side of his head a ruin.

And Bascomb had been wrong from the start, which made his dying even worse because he had thrown himself away, and it baffled Angevine, this thing in

169

men that made them do that.

Gore had done it by stubbornly refusing to accept the fact that the distant smoke had meant that Indians were about. And Holly had gone ahead and built something in his own mind until it possessed him.

And now Bascomb, proud, refined Resin Bascomb, who threw aside the fetters of discipline and went out like some ancient knight to do battle with the dragons, was slain by an overpowering desire to cover himself with distinction.

Loch Angevine didn't understand that, why a man would seek what he already had. Bascomb came from a good family, earned good marks at the Academy, and by his performance and attention to duty he had earned the respect of his superior officers. What more was there that a man needed?

Perhaps there was something in distinction that became habit-forming, something that pushed a man from glory to glory, using situations like stepping stones across an endless pond, for Angevine understood there was only one final resolution, to die bravely, die well, and thereby make the event important in the minds of other men.

Sergeant Gore hadn't died well, not really. He had died with the brass taste of fear in his mouth and the certain knowledge in his mind that his pride, his inability to admit ignorance, had brought him to this end.

And I put the glory to him, Angevine thought. *I made him important when he wasn't important at all.*

I gave meaning to something that had no significance.

But he knew he couldn't do it this time. He had survivors and wounded, but the dead they had left behind had to be accounted for.

When they rode into Tucson, everyone who saw them knew that they had taken a licking; it is in the way a man rides, carries his head, and in the look in his eye.

As soon as they reached the army encampment, Sergeant Angevine detailed the wounded to the surgeon's tent, then searched out the cavalry major. He did not have to search, for the major had viewed from the hotel the detail's return and hurriedly got his horse and went to the army camp in time to meet Angevine coming from the surgeon's tent.

He rushed up, angry, and then he saw Angevine's expression and looked at his eyes, and the major's manner changed. He spoke softly. "Come along, sergeant; I'll get you a drink and then we can talk."

As they went back to town, the major tried to remain silent, but he could not hold it back. "Bascomb is dead, I suppose?"

"Yes, sir."

"And the others?"

"Twelve died right off, sir. Four others on the way back."

"Over half," the major said, and Angevine looked at him and noticed that he had gray hair and tired lines around his eyes.

They dismounted in front of the hotel, and when

they passed through the lobby, the major spoke to the clerk. "Have a bottle and glasses brought to my room." They went up the stairs and he opened the door and took off his kepi and threw it casually on the bed. Then he spoke as he stripped off his gloves. "When I got here and found that Bascomb was gone, I imagined the worst. He went to Mexico?"

"Yes, sir."

"I was afraid of that. Well, if he'd lived I'd have court-martialed him as sure as you're standing there." He lit a cigar and looked at Sergeant Angevine. "You tried to dissuade him?"

"Yes, sir, several times. Lieutenant Bascomb was determined, sir."

The hotel clerk came up with the bottle of whisky and two glasses; the major took them and shoved the door closed with his toe. Then he poured and Angevine tossed his down. "Major," he said, "may I speak freely?"

"Of course. I want it that way."

"When Sergeant Gore was killed, it wasn't exactly like I reported. Fact is, sir, it wasn't like that at all. I saw smoke earlier that day and pointed it out to Gore, thinking it was Indians. Every time I heard a pack rat rustle, I just knew it was an Indian. Sergeant Gore thought the smoke was a dust devil. He could have been right, but he wasn't. The Apaches hit us at dawn and we didn't kill a single one of them. I don't think we fired more than four or five shots."

The major said nothing, just watched Angevine and

172

smoked his cigar. "Go on, sergeant."

"Somehow I survived that massacre, sir, but I did not report the true facts to Lieutenant Bascomb."

"Why not, sergeant?"

Angevine shrugged. "I think, sir, I could not bear the humiliation of admitting that we had been completely defeated, completely taken in. I can offer no other excuse." He waited for the major to say something, and when he didn't, Angevine went on. "I had already been inside Ortega's hacienda and I knew that he could defend it, and I'm sure he has from time to time fought off the Apaches from there. So when Lieutenant Bascomb wanted to raid Ortega's, I knew that he was heading for trouble. That and crossing the border."

"Why did he do it, sergeant?"

"Do you want an opinion, sir?"

"That's what I'm asking for."

"I think, sir, he just couldn't stand the thought of me disregarding orders and coming back a winner. I didn't go hunt the Pimas. I rode south, figuring I'd pick up Collins' Mexican contact. I think he believed he could wipe Ortega out and get away with it because you can't hardly hit a winner." He shook his head. "You could say, sir, that I'm responsible for him doing what he did."

"In a way you are, Angevine," the major said. He butted out his cigar and poured another drink. "Yet you did what you set out to do and Bascomb didn't. He left a mess for someone else to explain away, and

I'll tell you this: I'm not going to be able to explain what happened and have the general understand it." He wiped a hand across his face and stroked his splendid mustache. "Let me ask you a few questions. How many of the soldiers could swear that they were in Mexico?"

"I could, sir, because I knew we'd crossed the border. But the others wouldn't know. We crossed at night and got back before daylight."

The major nodded. "Angevine, I can't file a report saying that an armed military force crossed the border. I'm not going to throw away my career on a man who is already dead, a man I would court-martial were he alive to stand trial."

"What are you going to do, sir?"

"I'm going to lie, for the good of the service. And for your good, and mine, if you choose to think of it that way. I'm going to report the engagement as having taken place just this side of the border; we fought Mexican gun runners. Then I'm going to pray that the general accepts it and lets it go at that." He reached for the bottle again, then changed his mind. "Sergeant, you're an educated man and you ought to be more than a sergeant. The general would accept my recommendation to commission you a second lieutenant."

"Thank you, sir, but I'm not a leader."

"Neither was Bascomb, obviously, and you did get what was left of the command out of there." He held up his hand to cut off any possible interruption.

174

"Angevine, I don't intend to debate this. I'll wire the general right away and tomorrow morning you can turn in your report with a proper signature. Angevine, we all have a lot of work ahead of us and we'll never see our job finished because someone always comes up with a new one." He smiled and lit a fresh cigar. "Now I suggest that you get a bath and a shave and a haircut; I can't have a new junior officer going around with locks long enough to braid. And get rid of that outlandish fringed coat and Mexican sombrero. You're going to be an officer and a gentleman, Angevine."

"Yes, sir, but I'd be just as happy—"

"Soldier, I'm not a damned bit interested in your happiness. Good day now and I'll see your report in the morning."

He answered Angevine's salute then went and stood by the window and looked out, and he saw Angevine cross the street and go down to a Mexican barber shop. He felt fortunate in a way that Angevine had the education to qualify for a commission, for once he put his name on the report, the thing would be done and he could never go back on it.

And it was the only way to do it, for the good of the service, and perhaps a little bit for myself, he thought. Then he picked up his kepi, went down to the telegrapher's office, and composed his message very carefully.

He read it to make sure it said exactly what he wanted it to say:

Commanding General
Department of Platte
Fort Union, N. M. Terr.
Lt. Resin Bascomb killed line of duty . . . report
follows . . . Upon my recommendation, pending
your approval, Sgt. Loch Angevine appointed lieu-
tenant replacement . . . Angevine fully qualified.
Ronald Hoskins, Maj.
U. S. Cavalry

He was asking a favor of the general, not in so many words, but it was there, a request to endorse the promotion, and the general would grant it and remember it and someday the major would have to pay it back. But Hoskins was ready to do that; he was willing to deal to get out of this one.

It wasn't the first time and he supposed it would not be the last; this was so because he was human and the army was human, although no one ever acted as though they were. Like doctors, they were supposed to be perfect, to win every battle, to make every strategy brilliant, never stopping to consider that when someone wins, another loses.

If Resin Bascomb had lived, Hoskins knew that he would have nailed the lieutenant to the flagpole, but the man was dead and the mess had to be covered up for no other reason than that it just wasn't good to have civilians and newspapers writing about the military's biggest blunder of late.

He walked back to the hotel, thinking of Angevine;

they came out of nowhere, these men, and once in a while, amid the malcontents and the drifters and the trouble-makers, one rose like a Roman candle, briefly illuminating. Angevine was like that—seemingly quiet, average, yet he stood out like a shout.

Loch Angevine lounged in the barber's chair while the man snipped and trimmed and combed; he left generous sideburns and the mustache, which had grown to splendid proportions, but bladed the rest of Angevine's face clean.

Relaxed under the barber's hot towel, Angevine considered this last turn of events and genuinely wished that it hadn't happened. Somehow it seemed to be his destiny to be pushed into events before he was ready for them. His promotion to corporal had been unexpected and he would just as soon have passed it up, feeling that he needed more experience before accepting the responsibility. And he had felt the same way when he was made sergeant.

He wasn't a scout, but they had made him a scout anyway, and it seemed that he was always reaching to perform beyond the limit of his ability.

Now he was going to be a second lieutenant, an officer, and he was certain that this was not going to work out well at all, unless of course they sent him back to surveying, a safe occupation that he knew. He decided to speak to the major about that, for there were military posts to be built and such duty would take him out of the mainstream of trouble. Perhaps in a year or two, when he began to feel comfortable in his rank, he would accept more demanding duties.

Bathed and made presentable, Angevine paid the barber and left the shop. That afternoon he spent carefully wording his report to Major Hoskins; he rewrote it three times to get it exactly right, and when he was finished, anyone reading it would definitely place the action on the border, the exact location undefined, yet certainly on the United States side.

The major's orderly found him in the soldier camp; he came up and stood there as though trying to decide whether to salute or not. He handed Angevine a requisition slip. "Draw your uniform from Sgt. Burns at the supply tent. The major wants to see you right after—sir."

Angevine folded the report and put it in his pocket. "Did the major get a telegram from the general?"

"Yes, sir. You're the new lieutenant."

"Well, hold your congratulations," Angevine said and returned to town. As he walked down the street, shouldering his way through the sidewalk traffic, Angevine realized that his life had been drastically altered by the general's endorsement to Hoskin's recommendation, and he wasn't so sure that it was for the best.

He turned in at the large adobe that they kindly called a hotel, which was making do until someone put up a proper building. The downstairs was spacious, with a lobby and dining room, while on the second floor a hallway separated a row of dreary rooms with calcimined walls and spiders nesting in the roof beams.

Major Hoskins was on the porch; he took Angevine by the arm and led him aside to a bench where they could sit and talk. "I trust you have the report, lieutenant?"

"Yes, sir. I think you'll find it carefully worded." He gave it to the major, who read it meticulously, nodding and mumbling his approval.

"I'll send a rider east with a copy tonight, but I'll telegraph it to the general immediately. It may please you to know that I have been instructed to activate Camp Lowell on the east edge of town."

"Activate, sir? There's nothing there to activate."

Hoskins smiled. "You're going to build a post, Mr. Angevine. Specifications are on their way on the stage, so you might as well start surveying and preparing the ground immediately."

"We'll need equipment, sir. Fresno scrapers and—"

"Yes, I know. All this is being shipped to Fort Union. I want you to take a company and return there. You can bring the wagons back."

"Major, I can't survey the site and go to Fort Union at the same time. Perhaps one of your other officers—"

"Yes, yes, of course," Hoskins said with a trace of irritation. "After all, you're not cavalry and really not suited to a tactical command. Bascomb's idiocy has so thinned the Engineers that you may have difficulty finding a good crew."

"I'll train them, sir."

"Excellent," Hoskins said, smiling. "I trust you'll be suitably uniformed the next time I see you?"

"Yes, sir."

"You look better with your hair cut. Carry on, Mr. Angevine. Don't disappoint me now." He gave Angevine a friendly squeeze on the arm to tell him that "you're one of us," but warning him at the same time that people would be keeping their eyes on him.

Walking away, Angevine was unimpressed, and because of this, he was a bit disappointed. Hoskins, in many ways, was like Angevine's father, preaching perfection, and revealing small personal flaws, and that made it difficult for a man to steady down his respect and loyalty.

In the next few days he found time to select a proper site, pick a surveying crew, and commence work. Major Hoskins, along with one other officer and a company of cavalry, departed for Fort Union, leaving only an elderly senior lieutenant and the surgeon in command of what was left of Hoskin's force.

Since the army was spread miserably thin in the territory, Angevine wondered where the men would come from to occupy the posts that were to be built. But this was some general's worry and probably the army would come marching in, a column a mile long, and the general would figure that in numbers alone they'd scare the hell out of the Apaches and run them all on reservation.

Angevine didn't think so because he was learning that nothing is ever easy, and if something bad can happen, it usually will.

Time and trouble and work had put all thoughts of Colonel Bowen and his charming wife and daughter out of Angevine's mind, but these things were instantly recalled when the colonel and an entourage of four wagons and a full company rolled into town from the Camp Yuma road.

The colonel saw that Mrs. Bowen and her daughter were made comfortable; then he came on out to the camp site, bare ground with stakes driven here and there and covered with wax pencil markings, and he seemed very put out because progress had not advanced beyond this point.

Immediately he had the officer in charge summoned, and when Angevine came up, the colonel seemed even more annoyed.

"You enjoy rapid promotions, lieutenant," Bowen said. "No doubt due to your brilliant grasp of tactics." He slapped his gauntlets against his thigh. "May I ask the whereabouts of Major Hoskins?"

"Fort Union, sir. He's escorting equipment and wagons."

"Indeed? I expected him to return to Yuma. As it is, I had to leave the garrison in the command of a captain."

"That's a pity, sir. What is it the colonel wanted?"

"Well I damned well want to know why work hasn't progressed here." He looked around, his manner fretful. "Where the devil is Bascomb? He was supposed to have started construction a week ago."

"Lieutenant Bascomb is dead, sir." Angevine briefly explained the circumstances. "I've assumed his duties and responsibilities."

"I see. Very well. I'll remain here and assume command until Major Hoskins returns. Are there any other officers?"

"Yes, sir, a lieutenant of cavalry and the surgeon."

Bowen nodded. "I'll be at that pigsty you call a hotel. My wife is not feeling well you know. She plans to return east. The climate is too harsh for her delicate system."

"Delicate, sir?" He caught Bowen's sharp look and added, "I didn't know she was in poor health, sir."

"I trust the officers here will show her every courtesy during our stay, Mr. Angevine. You may present your cards this evening." He pulled on his gloves, then said, "Of course that was a figure of speech. You may call this evening in proper dress. I trust you will inform the others."

"Yes, sir."

He mounted and rode back to town, and Angevine went over to where Lieutenant McMasters and a cavalry detail were building a corral. When he told McMasters, the lieutenant swore in magnificent fashion, then smiled and promised to appear at the hotel that evening.

The contract surgeon, who had a tent full of wounded men, indicated that he had no damned inten-

182

tion of spending five minutes with that bitch or even saying hello and said that Angevine could quote him.

The survey crew worked until sundown, and it was well after nine o'clock before Angevine finished his bath and shave, changed into clean clothes, and made his way to town. Lieutenant McMasters had already gone in, two hours before, and on the way Angevine suspected that he had committed a grave social error and wondered how deeply he would regret it.

He found a place to tie his horse and ducked under the hitchrack and crossed the porch, stopping when a voice in the shadows said, "I don't think I'd go in there, lieutenant."

He peered and identified Eleanor Bowen; immediately he took off his kepi and stepped away from the light coming through the open door. "I should offer my apologies for being late," he said.

"That wouldn't do. Mother wouldn't accept them and Mr. McMasters would be angry because he had to dine alone." She giggled. "It's really a great deal for one junior officer to bear."

"You shouldn't talk like that," he said, trying not to sound as though he were reprimanding her.

"It's an attempt to stay honest. Won't you sit down?"

"Thank you, but I—"

"I wish you would. I've been waiting for you. Mother thinks I'm in my room with a headache."

He realized that he just couldn't stand there, so he sat down and stretched his legs. "I didn't think I'd ever see you again," he said.

"Did you want to?"

"Well, of course."

"You never acted like it. I've smiled at you and you didn't bat an eye."

"I hardly thought it was my place," Angevine said.

"You're not a sergeant now. Even Mother couldn't object."

He laughed. "Knowing your mother, I'm sure she'd find sufficient reason." Then he realized what he had said. "I'm sorry. I didn't mean to be critical."

"Oh, go ahead. She's a terror. Very unhappy with herself, and to keep from being lonely, she tries to make everyone else unhappy. It's strange, isn't it, that she devotes so much energy to it? She could go in the other direction and rise to everyone else's level."

"I'm afraid it's not proper to be sitting here analyzing her," Angevine said. "Certainly not for me, at any rate."

"I haven't told her yet," Eleanor said, "but I'm not going back east with her. I've decided to stay here and settle down with a husband. What do you think of that?"

"Well—it's a—a natural thing to do. You're a very pretty girl and—"

"And you think someone is a lucky man? Isn't that the standard reply?"

He frowned. "I think you're trying to argue with me."

"No I'm not. What do you think of marriage?"

"To be honest, I haven't thought much about it. I have problems of my own to resolve first."

184

"Such as?"

"Well, I'm not very sure of myself, you know. I'd like to gain confidence first."

"Confidence in what?"

She had the kind of a probing mind that made him feel defensive. He decided to change the subject. "Why don't you tell me about the young man you're going to marry?"

"All right. He's nice, mannerly when he wants to be. But he's a strong man, quite courageous."

"Of course he's army."

"Oh, yes. An officer."

Angevine was sorry he had introduced the subject. "I don't suppose I know him?"

"Yes you do," she said softly. "I've picked you, Loch."

He jumped to his feet. "But—you can't do a thing like that!"

"Yes I can. Does the idea bother you? I thought it might." She sounded delighted.

12

Lieutenant Loch Angevine could not say just when it was that his attention had turned from himself and focused on the outside world, nor exactly when he stopped fretting about what people thought of *him* and started wondering what people thought in general, and why. But it had happened. He found he was not pleased all the time, or even much of the time, but he was not disturbed by this.

Now he was an officer, had been for eleven days, and he knew every enlisted man on the post, which surprised him because he had always been terribly poor at names. Yet he knew this was not entirely true; he had the intelligence to remember names and he hadn't done so before because he hadn't felt any sense of responsibility about any man except himself.

The onus of command bothered him not at all and he gave orders correctly and efficiently without being sure that he was leading his men, for he stubbornly clung to the notion that a leader waved his saber and charged and the men followed this splendid example of military foolishness.

Without waiting for the Fresno scrapers to arrive, Angevine hired a crew of a hundred Mexican workers and with shovels they began to grade and level the site for the headquarters building while another crew made adobe.

Colonel Bowen daily put in his appearance and managed to suggest changes in just about everything; he felt that the buildings should face more to the south and left orders with Angevine to make the necessary changes. And Angevine went right ahead and raised the headquarters building exactly as indicated on the general plan set down by Major Hoskins.

Work kept Angevine busy from dawn to dark and he did not go to town unless he had to because he wasn't sure what he was going to do about Eleanor Bowen.

The thought of a woman pining for him gave him a feeling of superiority, but he did not feel at ease with her; she made him feel that he had to defend himself and he didn't like that and didn't think it should be that way.

Because he wanted to do his work correctly, Lieutenant Angevine applied himself diligently to every detail, however minor, and although he did not supervise the Mexicans directly, he took careful notice of them to make sure that none sat down on the job.

They had a tendency to look alike, with their dark faces and wide hats and white cotton shirts, but one drew his attention because he always turned away from Angevine. He did this so many times that Angevine became determined to find out why. So he got his horse and telescope and rode quite a distance away; then he dismounted and studied them carefully through the glass. It took him almost an hour to find the Mexican and then he studied the man for several minutes before he recognized him.

"Ortega!" he said, and quit looking through the telescope.

Conclusions came rapidly to Angevine: Ortega would not be alone; he wouldn't be able to do anything alone, so he must have quite a few men with him. This opened up other lines of reason; Ortega would not be here for any good-neighbor policy, so he had arms cached somewhere.

And he meant to use them.

The boldness of the man pleased Angevine; that was

walking into the jaws of trouble if a man ever did it. And of course Ortega would have Angevine marked for a bullet because he had crossed the Mexican and got away with it.

Still Angevine considered that he had the edge because he had taken his telescope and moved far enough away to be unobserved. Ortega would go on thinking that his presence was unnoticed, for he was known only to Angevine, and because of this he might bide his time, which Angevine could use.

Remounting, Angevine took the long way around and thereafter paid no special attention to Ortega or any of the other Mexicans. They had their own camp and spent their evenings there, laughing and singing and giving everyone the impression that they were a harmless, shiftless lot.

Mrs. Bowen, who was planning a social affair the likes of which Tucson had never seen, decided that it would be simply delightful to have those colorful natives play and entertain. Colonel Bowen was detailed to procuring them, a task he immediately assigned to Lieutenant Angevine.

At first thought, Angevine felt that he should object and tell the colonel exactly what was afoot, but knowing Bowen, he decided to keep this to himself. Since the *soirée* was yet three days away, this might give him time to scout out the arms cache, and while Ortega and band were doing the fandango for the gentry, Angevine and crew might take care of the guns.

The American-speaking leader was a man named Pedro Jiminez, and for ten dollars he agreed to have all of them in town at the appointed evening and there they would sing and entertain. This amused Angevine, having a man like Jiminez front for an aristocrat like Ortega, and he was once again reminded just how far a man will go to serve his own ends.

And Angevine had ends of his own to serve. Daily he took long hikes and once remained out overnight; he took nothing but his pistols and telescope on these jaunts, and he found what he wanted, about two miles south of the Mexican camp on a hillside in a natural cave.

Very carefully he made his plans and got the things he would need together, and he selected a cavalry sergeant, two corporals, and a horse holder to go with him.

They left camp on the evening of Mrs. Bowen's whoop-up, and Angevine realized that his absence would not be excused either by the colonel or his lady. And even Eleanor might find it difficult to understand. Still he had his obligations, his duty, and in the company of the enlisted men he rode south. Finally the sergeant, who was suspicious of all officers not wearing crossed sabers on their kepis, said, "Sir, would you mind tellin' me where we're going and what we're doing with lanterns and tools when it's going to be dark in thirty minutes?"

"We're going to make some alterations on some firearms, sergeant."

"Yes, sir." The sergeant looked at Angevine as though he now had living proof of what too much sun could do to a man.

They were in no hurry and it was twilight when Angevine stopped and ordered them to dismount. He gave the horses to the horse holder and motioned for them to take the sacks of tools and to follow him.

They made their way carefully, slowly along a rocky trail that would have terrified a goat, and then Angevine stopped. He turned to the sergeant and two corporals and said, "About a hundred yards farther on is a cave. The Mexicans have their rifles and ammunition hidden in there. I expect there is a guard whom we'll have to take care of. Sergeant, can you handle a knife?"

"Yes, sir. You want him slit or stuck?"

"I'm sorry to say that he'll have to be done in," Angevine said. "Can't afford a witness to tonight's work. Everything depends on it."

"I'll take care of it," the sergeant said, and opened a huge clasp knife. "I'll whistle when it's clear."

"All right." He turned to one of the corporals. "You bring up one of the horses when the sergeant signals. Take the Mexican to hell and gone away from here and pile a lot of rocks on him. You ought to finish before morning. Go right on back to camp and keep your mouth shut."

The corporal didn't grasp the significance of this, but he was certain that the evening wasn't going to be dull; he nodded and the matter was settled and the

190

sergeant went on afoot.

They waited for ten minutes; it seemed longer to Angevine and he wondered if he shouldn't have done this job himself. Then the sergeant whistled and the corporal took his horse and led him on ahead and they followed. The corporal was loading the Mexican across the saddle when they came up to the dark cave.

"Take the lanterns inside and light them," Angevine said, and carried in the tools. He laid everything out as soon as the lanterns spread a warm yellow light: hammers, files, screwdrivers, chisels, and a broom with the handle cut off.

Rifles and ammunition were stacked against one wall and the sergeant said, "Now who the hell would ever have thought it. They plannin' a little war, lieutenant?"

"Hardly a peace parley. Now this is what we're going to do. The Mexicans mean to surprise us. All right, let them. Only I want every firing pin on those Henry repeaters filed off. Do you see what I'm getting at? I don't want to take the rifles and have them go back to Mexico so they can get more and hit us again. I want them to attack and get cut up badly with rifles in their hands that won't fire. I want Ortega to think long and hard about ever coming back, if he's lucky enough to live through it. Understand now?"

The sergeant smiled. "Yes, sir. They'll never know we've been here. I see what the broom is for, to wipe out our tracks."

"Exactly. Each rifle will be put back exactly as it's

found. Now let's get to work."

Angevine had taken his own Henry rifle and studied it so that he knew exactly how to go about this; he demonstrated to the sergeant and they rendered each gun unfireable without doing anything to the outward appearance.

By working without let up, they completed the job in four hours, then carefully destroyed evidence of their visit, took tools and lanterns, and moved outside, blowing out the lights before leaving the mouth of the cave.

Angevine moved them back to where the horses were being held, and he brushed out their tracks carefully. When they reached the horses, the sergeant was cocking his head to one side and holding up his hand, and then Angevine heard what had taken his attention, the soft run of Spanish on a better trail below.

They squatted down and watched as about twenty of the Mexicans moved toward the cave, and then Ortega called out for the guard but got no answer.

There was a lot of talk, some argument, and the sergeant spoke in Angevine's ear. "I make out some of it, sir. They're cussin' the guard, figurin' he left his post."

"Let's get out of here," Angevine suggested. "Tonight's the night. I should have guessed it. Half of Tucson will be drunk or too tired to wake up."

The Mexicans were in the cave and making a lot of noise, so they mounted up and worked back to where the trail was better, then rode at a trot until they

192

approached the silent army tents.

As the horse holder led the animals away, Angevine said, "Sergeant, quietly wake the men and have them remain in their tents, armed and ready. Fire on my command or when I commence firing. But it is important that Ortega think he's caught us asleep. Understand?"

"Yes, sir, I sure do." He grinned. "You're all right, sir, figuring all this out."

"You might be wise to spare the congratulations until later, sergeant."

Angevine went to his tent and got his Henry rifle and a belt of ammunition; he checked it to make certain that it was fully loaded, then he stretched out and waited, watching from under a slightly raised side of the tent.

The sergeant came around, moving like a ghost; he had the bugler with him. "Sir, you just give him your order and he'll toot it out proper for you."

"Thank you, sergeant. Return to your post."

After he left, Angevine looked at the boy and said, "What can you play on that, son?"

"Charge, retreat, as skirmishers—you name it, sir."

"I think tonight we'll use 'charge,' " Angevine said, with considerable satisfaction.

He kept watch and finally the Mexicans came, moving in carefully like shadows. Angevine let them come on in close, in among the tents for the Mexicans wanted to make a massacre of this. He saw Ortega, now only ten feet away, and Angevine decided that it was time. "Sound the charge," he said, and bounded from the tent as Ortega pulled the trigger.

The brass voice of the bugle cut the silence and across Ortega's face came a look of shocked surprise as the rifle failed to fire. Loch Angevine said, "Goodbye, señor gun runner," and shot. The bullet hit the Mexican a bit off center, spinning him slightly, then the legs bent like softening wax, and he fell as soddenly as thrown mud.

The camp was a fury of gunfire as the soldiers cut the Mexicans to pieces; there was no escape for them and many threw their useless firearms aside and flung up their hands.

"Sound the cease fire!" Angevine yelled, and the bugler took it up and the shooting died off.

The sergeant and six men immediately herded the remaining Mexicans into a huddle and gestured for them to throw their firearms down, which they did. Six of the Mexicans, including Ortega, were dead and a few of the survivors were wounded; the rest stood with their hands high. Angevine had lanterns brought up and he singled out Jiminez, whom one of the troopers shoved away from the others.

Angevine pointed to Ortega and said, "He is dead. See? Ortega is dead. No more guns will be sold to the Indians. Understand?"

He did not tell them about working on their guns because he wanted them to wonder about it, to brood; he told the sergeant to gather every Mexican rifle and belt of ammunition and to place them under guard for the remainder of the night.

He summoned a corporal. "I want all their horses rounded up and held. Put a strong guard over them. The prisoners will be guarded here tonight."

There was a rush on the town road and then Colonel Bowen and the cavalry lieutenant came up and flung off their horses; Bowen, being a bit more bulky, did it less gracefully.

"What is the meaning of this?" Bowen demanded. "What is going on here? Angevine, I demand an explanation!"

"And you shall have it, sir," Angevine said, taking him by the flabby arm. "This dead man is Ortega, sir, who was responsible for the death of Lieutenant Bascomb and the others. He is a gun runner, sir, and has made a good deal of money selling firearms to the Indians."

Bowen's mouth got round and he stared at Ortega, then at Angevine. "I once visited Ortega's hacienda, sir, and a few days ago I recognized him but did not let him know it. He was disguised as a worker, sir, beard, dirty face, and all."

"Why wasn't I informed of this?"

"Sir, you were occupied with Mrs. Bowen's social success. I didn't want to interrupt the colonel."

"You're being flippant!"

"Then I beg your pardon, sir," Angevine said. "However, I reasoned that if Ortega were here, he did not mean to punish us with a switch, and since any display of firearms around the post would have raised suspicions, I concluded that they were cached. Fortunately, I found them, and with some help, we altered the weapons so they would not fire."

Bowen began to grasp it. "Why, these men attacked in the jaws of certain death!" He showed outrage. "That's neither civil nor sporting, Angevine. A man deserves a fighting chance."

Recalling the cannon and the grapeshot that had killed and maimed at the main gate that dawn, Angevine said, "I was not inclined to play games, sir. Neither did I want Ortega to retreat to strike again some other time."

"My God, you got him cold," Bowen said. "But what are we going to do with the others? We can't try and hang them!"

"No, sir, I realize that's not practical. However, we can guard them until the post is built, then escort them to the border. That is, unless the colonel wishes to make adobe brick himself."

"You're getting flip again," Bowen warned. Then he wiped his mouth and thought about it. "I suppose you're right." He looked at McMasters. "Haven't you anything to say, Phillip?"

"No, sir. It seems that Mr. Angevine has the situation well in hand." He winked at Angevine. "And frankly, sir, I don't see how you can avoid writing him up for this. Considering that he's not even cavalry." He laughed in his chest, a soft rumble. "Missed you at the party, Loch; it was quite an affair."

"By the way—" Bowen began, then closed his

mouth with a snap. "Never mind. I want a written report by ten o'clock, Mr. Angevine." He glanced at McMasters. "Will you take charge here, Phil? I want a word in private with Mr. Angevine."

"Certainly, sir." He saluted, turned, and walked off.

Bowen pulled at his lip. "My daughter is quite angry with you, sir. Failing to appear the way you did."

"I'm sorry to hear that, sir."

"What are your intentions?"

"Intentions? Frankly, colonel, to stay as far away from your daughter as I can."

Bowen reared back. "What?"

"Try to understand, sir. I mean no slight against your daughter, but I would prefer to select my own wife, not have her chosen for me. And meaning no disrespect, I feel your wife and I would not grow congenial with the years, and Eleanor, being a chip off the old block so to speak, would naturally side with her mother."

"You're bordering on the insulting, sir!" Then he waved his hand. "However, that's not the point. Eleanor has confessed to me that she has fallen in love with you."

"I'm afraid she doesn't know what it is, sir."

"And you do? You're a man of the world? Dammit—" He stopped and blew out a long breath. "All right, Angevine, all right. She did the same thing back east, you know. Put the officer in one devil of a spot. And my wife stuck her spoon in and damned near ruined his career. Made everyone think the poor devil had gotten Eleanor in a family way. Not true, of course. But the talk was there." He shrugged. "I've always been cursed by women, Angevine. The only boy among seven sisters. They can bully a man something dreadful. My father went to an early grave; I've always thought the Lord took pity on him."

"I'm sorry you've had disappointing experiences, sir, but the fact remains that I have no intention of keeping company with Eleanor or courting her in any way. I might suggest, sir, that Eleanor means to remain here. She says so anyway."

"Yes, until the next attractive man comes along." He smiled. "When they return east, do you think Mr. McMasters would be suitable as an escort?"

"He's very tall and quite dashing, sir. A bachelor too."

"Ah, so he is. And he danced several times with Eleanor tonight." Bowen smiled. "I'd feel so much better if she were married. Let some other man have the responsibility. Why be selfish, I say. Don't you agree?"

"Yes, sir. And perhaps Mrs. Bowen would spend at least half of the year with her daughter and husband."

"Aaaaahhh, blessed thought. I like you, Mr. Angevine. A clear head. Right to the point." He smiled and clasped Angevine on the arm. "Naturally, if Mr. McMasters and my daughter were to marry, I'd want him transferred east. Be more comfortable for Eleanor."

"Yes, sir. And farther away too."

"Aaahhaaa, you grasp the situation completely." He chuckled and took out two cigars. Angevine took one and the light, feeling as he did so that it was apt to make him sick. "You won't let on to McMasters, will you?"

"No, sir, I'd want him to be surprised."

He turned to his horse and huffed himself into the saddle, then waved and turned back toward town. Angevine watched him go, then went over to the command tent where McMasters was giving orders to the sergeant.

The man walked off as Angevine came up and McMasters smiled. "Cady has been relating the events to me. Very thorough job, Mr. Angevine. You're apt to make a promotion in five or six years at that rate."

"To tell you the truth, sir, I'm pretty satisfied with things just the way they are."

McMasters laughed and stroked his mustache. "You and the major had quite a little chat over there. Did I hear him laughing?"

"Yes, he's a jolly soul once you get to know him."

McMasters rolled his eyes heavenward. "Mrs. Bowen was as sweet as pie tonight, the center of attention." He thumped Angevine on the arm. "I—ah, wasn't too sorry you didn't show up, Loch. That Eleanor is a looker all right."

"Very nice girl. Sweet disposition."

"I've been meaning to ask you. You guided them over the pass, didn't you? Made a damned hero of yourself too, I understand."

"It wasn't much," Angevine said. "Eleanor's a gentle girl, you know, very sensitive. Some man will just sweep her off her feet one of these days. That's the way they go, fast and final."

"Yes," McMasters said seriously. "But I've always held that a woman like that needs a mature man. You agree?"

"Oh, yes."

McMasters laughed. "Nothing against you, Loch— you know I like you and you're coming along—but you're too young for her. I hope you don't take offense."

"No, not at all. Excuse me, I see a detail I should attend to." He dashed off to the other side of the camp, then sat down on a pile of adobe brick and smiled because for the first time in his life he felt completely equal to any man and a little bit superior to most, particularly Lucius Bowen and Phil McMasters.

Let them strut and preen and posture; he understood them now and Bowen's uncertainties had no effect on him, and never would again. Why, Angevine thought, I could serve under him now and not be bothered a bit. And as he thought that, he realized that now he could go back home; he even felt the desire to go back, a gentle pulling that would get stronger as the days passed.

Going back home was nice to think about.

13

Adobe construction has two things in its favor: it is fast going up, and it is durable, especially in predominantly dry, hot climates, and Arizona Territory qualified on both counts. The headquarters building was doorless and windowless when Major Ronald Hoskins returned with earth-moving equipment and eight wagons, yet he was immensely impressed for he had expected to see no construction at all, just a flurry of survey stakes.

The soldiers were busy making door frames and windows, and Hoskins found that he could move into the building and occupy it while it was being finished, which pleased him so much that he maintained a good humor while Colonel Bowen bombarded him with endless gossip.

Hoskin's first act was to relieve Bowen of further responsibility so he could return to Camp Yuma. Since Bowen's wife and daughter, in the company of Lieutenant McMasters, were on their way east, a new sense of purpose came over the command.

Since the soldiers had learned how to make adobe bricks, the Mexicans were discharged and escorted back to the border. Hoskins didn't want them around, figuring that once there had been trouble, it might flare up again.

So through the winter and into spring Angevine worked to erect the post, and when he was finished, there was a neatly laid out parade ground, sutler's store, quartermaster buildings, barracks, officers' row, and all the small outbuildings necessary to service the three companies that were scheduled to arrive in March.

Rumor had it that the entire military force in Arizona was due for a strengthening and a full scale campaign instigated to put down the Apaches, who really hadn't been bothersome that winter, but who ought to be confined to a reservation just on general principles.

Generals in Washington, along with officials of the Department of Indian Affairs, had selected a site for the reservation, which would be called the San Carlos, and Hoskins had been placed in charge of building a headquarters, with a schedule of completion set for sometime in the late fall.

And in accord with the military policy of rewarding a good job by piling on more work, Lieutenant Angevine was assigned the task of surveying the reservation.

Immediately realizing the enormity of the assignment, Angevine requested that he be granted forty-five days leave, and the major, seeing no immediate rush to do anything, granted it.

The stage was getting through regularly, although the shotgun guard was ever alert and all male passengers were requested to travel heavily armed; Angevine immediately bought his ticket and left Tucson within two days. Which was fortunate, for Lieutenant McMasters' request for transfer to a post in Ohio came through and Hoskins had to sign it or come up with a lot of reasons why not, and he was suddenly quite shy of junior officers. He could have appealed to Colonel Bowen for a temporary assignment, but he wanted to owe the colonel no favors.

Hoskins considered recalling Angevine by telegraph. Hoskins weighed the matter and decided that a disappointed lieutenant was worse than none at all. After all, it would only be forty-five days and then he'd have Angevine back and Hoskins had to admit that there was nothing finer for a commander than a good, reliable, level-headed second lieutenant. You could exact the best duty from them for years by dangling promotion just out of reach. Hoskins decided against recalling Angevine immediately.

Riding east on the stage, Lieutenant Angevine was amazed that he had not seen this country before, since he had once passed through it. Daily he bounced and rocked along in the sultry heat and coughed at the dust and enjoyed every bit of it. He was surprised to find that men had heard of him and they spoke with respect, for he had a bit of a reputation now; these westerners spoke politely to any man who had drawn Apache blood.

Through New Mexico the stage ran northeast and met, finally, the railroad as it passed through Kansas. There Angevine stayed over night at a fine hotel, ate his dinner with a napkin tucked into the throat of his tunic, and enjoyed the luxury of a barber's attention.

Train fare was not inexpensive, but he was an officer and the conductor fixed him up with a compartment all the way to Chicago, and there was no extra charge for this. Angevine realized that this was purely the conductor's doing, and at one of the stops, he bought the man a box of fine Havana cigars and gave them to him before he left the train.

A night train out of Chicago rushed him across the rolling land of Indiana and into Ohio. He got off early the next morning, hired a buggy and driver for the eighteen mile ride, and settled back in the seat, feeling a dry nettle stinging on the back of his neck. He could not recall feeling this excitement before, for in leaving he had felt no sense of loss, no sense of detachment.

When they neared his hometown, he directed the driver along a county road until they came to a lane shaded by trees just threatening to bud. He got down, took his bags, paid the driver, and watched the rig turn and disappear down the road.

Angevine looked at the vast fields, yet unturned by spring plowing, and down at the end of the lane the great house where he had been raised. It surprised him to find that he could recall no unhappiness at all and he wondered if he had ever been unhappy living there or had just imagined it.

Picking up his bags, he walked on down the lane, and as he drew nearer, a large dog pounded out, barking in a deep rumble, and then the dog came close, sniffed, and sat down in the lane and looked puzzled.

"Scots," Angevine said and the dog's ears twitched, then the tail wagged and it bounded up, paws against his chest. As he walked on, the dog raced about, barking, setting up a happy clamor. Then the front door opened and Angus Angevine stepped out onto his wide porch.

He looked at Loch as he came up the path, boots crunching cinders in the carriage drive. Then the old man said, "Me wee bairn, if ye're not a bonnie sight!"

Loch said, "You don't look any older, father."

"Come in. Set yer bags down. They can be fetched later." He took his youngest son by the arm and opened the door for him. "Stuart and Dundee are home. Robert is whalin' somewhere in the watery parts of the world." He paused in the hallway. "Stuart! Dundee! Come see what the wind's blown in!"

After the dinner that evening, when they sat around the great table, Loch Angevine realized that for the first time he did not want to be excused, to remove himself from the company of these men who shared his blood.

Stuart, growing gray now, with deep lines around his eyes, still boomed out his words as though he talked against the roar of a tempest. Dundee, the cocky one with the temper, still had a certain wildness about him, but it didn't frighten Loch Angevine at all.

And the laird himself, Angus Dundee, sat at the head of the table, bursting with questions, and Loch Angevine feared none of them now.

"An officer," Angus said. "Tis a grand thing to make such a mark. Wouldn't ye say so, Stuart?"

"Aye." He smiled. "Ye've done brave things, lad, to gain such a rank. But ye're home to stay now."

"I have to report back to my post in forty-five days," Loch said.

Angus showed his surprise. "But ye've done what ye set out to do, lad. What's to go back to? This is your home!"

"Father, I found out something in the Indian country. I understand now that I wasn't doing anything for you. It was for myself, so I'm going back there. It's a life I want. I like it. When I can, I'll come back to visit. But that's all."

"Tell us a tale or two," Stuart urged. "I've sailed into a port or two myself since we last met." He winked and smiled.

"Aye," Angus said, adding his urging. "Tell us how you came to be an officer, lad."

Angevine looked at his father, then at his brothers, and said, "By being a little brave once in a while. And by being afraid a lot of the time. And lying when I thought I had to. And honest a few times when it hurt." He paused and looked at them, waiting for them to say something.

Stuart said, "That's not a thing I wanted to hear, boy."

"No, but it's as good as all the tales you've told and I listened to," Loch said flatly.

The older brother started to bristle and his eyes

206

turned chilly. "Would you call me a liar then?"

"No, but none of it really happened the way you've told it." He glanced at his father and at Dundee. "I don't know the real straight of what's happened to me, so I say that I don't think things happened the way you say at all. Wouldn't you agree?" Stuart started to rise out of his chair, but old Angus put a clamping hand on his forearm and held him. Loch continued to look steadily at Stuart; then he smiled and said, "So I've come back for a visit and we can sit around and swap tall stories, the way you always used to. Or you can take exception to what I've said. All right?"

For a moment there was complete silence, then Dundee roared with laughter and beat his hand on the table and old Angus took it up and the frigidity left Stuart's face and was replaced with a smile and laughter.

He sat down and reached for the bottle and said, "Lad, you've learned more than I reckoned you would."

Old Angus reached for the bottle. "We'll hae a drink or two t'that," said he, and he poured first for his youngest son.

Loch Angevine was home.

THE END

Center Point Publishing
600 Brooks Road ● PO Box 1
Thorndike ME 04986-0001 USA

(207) 568-3717

US & Canada:
1 800 929-9108

Ns